The
House
of
Pearl

Robert Max Bovill
Susan B. Flanagan

iUniverse, Inc.
Bloomington

THE HOUSE OF PEARL

iUniverse books may be ordered through booksellers or by contacting:

iUniverse
1663 Liberty Drive
Bloomington, IN 47403
www.iuniverse.com
1-800-Authors (1-800-288-4677)

ISBN: 978-1-4759-8234-3 (sc)
ISBN: 978-1-4759-8236-7 (hc)
ISBN: 978-1-4759-8235-0 (e)

Library of Congress Control Number: 2013905721

Printed in the United States of America

iUniverse rev. date: 4/18/2013

"The story is so unique and so elegantly stitched together that there was never a dull moment. The many fascinating characters that kept coming and going and all of the exotic locations they visited kept me turning the pages. If George were alive today we would have truly enjoyed reading this book to each other."

George C. Scott's widow,
Actress, Trish Van Devere

Acknowledgment

We wish to thank C. Phillips for her contributions.

Also in the works:

Be prepared for more amazing tales from Bovill/Flanagan

To our parents, whose love and support made everything possible by allowing us to chase our dreams, Josephine, Ted, Arlene and Paul.

Chapter 1

*T*he crowd at the stadium roared for another encore, but she was done. The chants of "ELIA, ELIA, ELIA!!!" echoed through the corridors of the stadium, rumbling the walls and becoming almost deafening.

One year on the road, and this was the last night of her latest tour, and she was tired: mentally and physically. The tall, dark haired singer rounded the corner to her dressing room and scurried down the cavernous hallways that run through the backstage of the stadium, she was followed by her entourage which rushed to keep up with her long-legged strides: agents, managers, stylists, her band, and autograph seekers all bustled behind her. She finally arrived at her dressing room and slammed the door on all of them, stopping them all in their tracks. *Alone at last.*

Elia Pearl was a big star now. She had four songs on the Billboard Top Ten, she had made millions, and she was a respected singer and songwriter. Her concerts sold out everywhere. She even had a song that was the new ad campaign for a huge retail chain. She should be on top of the world, but as she stared at her own deep green chain in her mirror, all she could feel was her own loneliness. In these quiet moments by herself, it almost consumed her, and nothing ever worked to heal the emptiness she felt every day: not the men, not the drinking, not the work. *Nothing.* She had no family to speak of, and outside of those people who worked for her or wanted something from her, she had no real true friends. It was a moment she replayed day in and day out.

As she sat down in her large make-up chair, she looked at herself in the mirror, surrounded by the bright bulbs; she wondered what was it all for? Who cared? Did she help people with her music or was it all just for fun and nothing deeper, more meaningful? She mindlessly looked around the table at the items scattered about: a hair brush, make-up removers, eyelashes, powder, lipstick—and an envelope addressed to her, Elia Pearl. Her eyes opened widely at this unexpected intrusion. She looked around to see who had left it, or how it got there, but the letter just sat there as if it had appeared out of nowhere.

The envelope was made of elegant parchment, with a golden family crest embossed on the top left corner. The handwriting was purposeful and the calligraphy impeccable. She opened the envelope to reveal a letter of the same quality paper. The letter was hand-written in an old-school script, you could tell it was an elderly person who had written it; Elia just knew exactly who it was from. *Rose, Rose Standish. How did she find me?* She shook her head and began reading:

> *My Dear Prima,*
>
> *I hope this letter finds you well; it has been many years since we have seen each other, and I think fondly of you and your lovely grandmother every day.*
>
> *Please excuse this intrusion, but I must ask your assistance with the house. It has fallen into disrepair and I hope that you will reconsider selling the property. It would fetch a vast sum, due to its location.*
>
> *We realize that it has been many years since you have returned, and I wanted to personally express*

my willingness to help you dispose of the property as you wish.

Of course, we would prefer that you come back home to care for the house, as it holds your family name and maybe you can build a life here.

Most Sincerely,
Rose Standish, Realtor and Your Friend

The house, *that house*, Elia had spent the last 20 years running away from it, and now it beckoned to her again. Years earlier, she had vowed she would never go back, and yet, she was drawn back to the place that had twisted the souls of so many unfortunate people.

Sausalito, San Francisco, Northern California—*home*? Maybe, if there ever was a time for her to go back, it was now. Maybe this was the time for her to do it, once and for all, to deal with her demons and her past. Go back to the house. Back to *that* house, back to the House of Pearl.

Elia thought long and hard, there were so few reasons to go back, and so many reasons to stay away. The lies, the betrayals and the sadness: sad—and evil—tragic events, things that had coursed through her family for generations. Maybe the evil was finally done with them. But like a moth to a flame, the urge to go back was too strong for Elia: she picked up her cell phone and texted her agent to get her on the first flight out and get her to San Francisco the next morning.

Chapter 2

$\mathcal{T}$he morning sun shone on the old window that needed urgent repair. One could see the paint had peeled and it was a shame to view the grandeur of this old home being neglected. Elia would soon arrive here and begin her own journey of discovery.

A ray of sunlight streamed in through the old window and then flickered menacingly through the long forgotten rustic floor. Below the floor a glistening streak of light wrapped itself around the contours of a mummified human head. One meandering line of light, similar to a Navy Seal's zigzagging war paint, revealed a pair of sunken, dead eyes. This once vibrant head, frozen in time, looked up toward the cracks in the floorboards. From what one could see in this dark underbelly of the house, was the side of its mouth, jaw opened wide as though it was staring up at its assassin with its face reflecting the final agony of its brutal end. Who was this man? Why had no one noticed the demise of this victim? His eyes, black and lifeless, glare longingly with no presence of life remaining within them. An unknown soul lost under these floorboards for decades. Yet there seemed to be a secret story hidden behind his dead, penetrating gaze.

Something prowled across the floorboards and followed the sun. A robust overfed Tabby cat began searching the floorboards for a warm spot to curl up on. It circled where the sunlight was streaming in. Below the floorboards like a Hollywood searchlight, the intense sunshine wrapped itself around the lifeless head as the nervous feline scratched at the floor and acutely sensed that something was amiss under these old shrunken and separated floorboards. As more was uncovered, one could see more, the tortured man's long ponytail seemed weirdly and pristinely preserved. There seemed to be no damage or any loss of characteristics that this man's once living face would have possessed. From what anyone could see, he was well preserved and attired in clothing from an era long since relegated to history books. Taking a closer look one could see his expression, still frozen on his lifeless face. The final emotion of fear was on his face, written for others to see, what he had been through the moment his life was so mercilessly taken.

The internal parts of his pitiful head suffered the attack of parasites and worms eating at it, but its external stare still looked up through the floorboards, where the cat still watched.

It must have been a terrorizing death. His face depicted the open frightful stare of a condemned man, frozen in shock. How was he murdered and how could this oddly attired man, still be preserved here beneath the floorboards? His demise left him utterly alone, his hidden presence known to no one other than this chubby cat. The strangest and eeriest part of this murdered man was not that he was dead, but under the surface it seemed as if something was different... something was unnatural. It seemed also by viewing him that something was buried within him: *something dark and unable to rest.*

A glint of precious gems appeared as the cat moved and the sun seeped in between the floorboard cracks again, and bounced off a blood red ruby. It was the handle of a very special, ancient Samurai Sword! There wasn't just one ruby but seventeen stunning rubies that ran up the handle, imbedded into the golden cording to aid a hand with its grip; it was an amazing piece of work. Why was it rammed down this poor soul's mouth? Who had owned this meticulously detailed, ornate and valuable weapon? It was obviously a rare work of art, a museum piece, the embossed designs and carvings on it were stunning, depicting intricate details of an era long past. Whoever owned this sword had not been overly concerned about losing such an exquisite item.

The sword was deeply plunged into the corpse's throat with only the ruby encrusted handle rising above. The handle was clean and shiny as if still in its own place and time. Mysteriously in the filthy crawlspace of this old bayside Victorian the sword had somehow remained pristine. There was no dust covering it and time had not worn or tarnished it. Proud of its accomplishment, the sword's handle refracted the sun's light into red and white beams that spread in all directions around the mummified head, as if it were holding it down; its victim still swallowing the razor like blade. Scrolling was revealed along its folded steel blade and an intricate dragon design was etched into the handle. This dragon etching displayed aggression, showing an unusual manifestation of two dragons wrapped around the hand guard, one consuming a Samurai and one disgorging a Samurai that was being reborn within the fire discharging from its mouth. Maybe it was a symbol of power and reincarnation. Either way, it was intricately created on the handle's guard for others to fear and see. The handle was wrapped with golden cord with what appeared to be small diamonds encircling each ruby. Each samurai is attired in his traditional fighting costume. Strangely enough, this particular sword tells more about the assassin than its victim.

The old white "Cottage Style" Victorian, with its rustic floorboards and with its hidden murdered body, seemed to be a home with numerous secrets and unusual happenings. This abandoned portion of the house had more crates than you could imagine. They seemed to be stacked uncaringly everywhere throughout the dusty abandoned apartment, which created the perfect playpen for the lazy Tabby to get into trouble. Some crates were open with their contents spilled out, while others seemed sealed and closed for many years.

Antique furniture bordered the walls, some covered with sheets, others not, with draping made of dust-covered sheets. There was so much dust that it truly was an unnatural occurrence for the old sword to be so clean. Some of the furniture was totally covered with layers of thick dust, but not the sword.

There were stacks of books piled on fragile shelves and old used nautical gear was hung on the walls and piled high in the corners and out on the floor.

Above a pile of ropes and turnbuckles a cracked stained-glass window allowed the outside sunlight to faintly shine through. The artwork of this stained-glass window was of a nineteenth century merchant schooner with what appeared to be Japanese calligraphy. The colors of the window were vibrant with deep reds, greens, blues and yellows. Part of the calligraphy and bow of the ship were broken out of the window. Aside from the nautical gear there was also the presence of more crates, boxes and lumber.

Cobwebs covered most of the room and there were doll's arms, heads, and bodies spilling out over the steamer trunks. In the back of the room many exotic musical instruments could be seen. There was an antique Japanese harp and it was still tightly strung. There was a banjo, a bamboo flute, an old Spanish guitar, various harmonicas and castanets, hand drums of various sizes that were meticulously made with high quality materials with inlays of pearls and jewels that seemed, after many years, to be in perfect condition.

Lying against one of the walls were worn-out and battered picture frames displaying unknown families. These pictures covered maybe seventy or one hundred year's span of time. Some seemed to be from the nineteen fifties and sixties. The dusty room housed collectables and paraphernalia from many eras.

Some objects were thousands of years old and others were only a few decades old. It was a strange home to say the least. A large oil painting, laid on its side, still glossy from the quality of oils used to paint it, was of a nude woman.

Eventually the curious Tabby found its way into the upstairs room and began searching through the empty home; it scurried down the hallway where framed sketches and large portraits covered the walls. These golden-framed portraits had revealed a history of seamanship. One of them depicted a strikingly handsome merchant captain of a large sailing vessel.

Many of the sketches and paintings showed places and had descriptions etched in small brass tags below on their frames: such places as Europe, Hawaii, India, Japan, Russia and South America. Next to the handsome captain was a painting of a beautiful Japanese woman who was oddly enough dressed in Annie Oakley Buckskins. The brass plate on the picture frame read, "My Precious Pearl."

Next to her the merchant captain stood proud in his portrait and had a handsome appeal about him, as one could see by the many worldly artifacts surrounding him. A bountiful display of natural pearls was front and center. On his left ring finger is a gigantic black Baroque Pearl, and in his raised left hand he held a magnificent strand of black and white pearls. He was dressed as a late nineteenth century salty merchant sea captain and below his portrait it read "Edwin 'The Pearl' Harrison, 1878." He was stately in his nautical uniform and his possessions shone brightly around him, including the very same Samurai sword that was shoved down the throat of the hapless corpse under the house. Even though he appeared strong and stern, there seemed to be a hint of sadness in his eyes.

You could hear the wind blowing around and through this old house and the creaking was loud and seemed as if the creaking was its own voice. The house made sounds as if it was a sigh, and it spoke its own language. Something wasn't normal about this home.

$$\text{⚓}$$

The three back bedrooms of the upper portion of the house were closed up with padlocks and abandoned. The long central hallway below the Tabby's entrance window, stretched toward the front of the house. Oddly enough, there was a ladder in the middle of the hallway that rose up to the attic. In the living room, there was a player piano and an eclectic collection of furniture. A bed built up on stilts in what was the dining room seemed to attain an outstanding view of the Bay Bridge, Alcatraz and the famous city's skyline.

The exterior view was scenic and serene, but the interior of this home told a whole different story. A story perhaps foretold by the eerily enticing waves that crashed on the rock seawall across the street in front of this 120-year old Victorian home.

The only person that was to be in this home today was Elia. The singer was on her way to take care of it, or possibly sell it, and if things go well, stay longer: she would remain open-minded and would see what happened.

She knew that the house was in disrepair from neglect over time, and she would find that her inheritance might have grand old world beauty, but as yet unknown to her, it still held a secret danger under its floorboards. She was bravely returning to this old Victorian home laced with supernatural occurrences from years earlier: occurrences that could have ended her young life at the time. The new activities would change her comfortable yet lonely lifestyle as a worldwide popular singer. A lifestyle she was used to... and sort of liked it just the way it was.

As a famous singer, Elia's voice was adored by her many fans and she was definitely a very striking woman to look at: her skin was fair and seemed to appear baby soft, with the elegance of a well-groomed woman. Elia's long black hair reached nearly to the base of her back, and its straight, thick and smooth textured, it always looked beautiful and she usually let it hang loose over her shoulders. Her black hair in the sunlight resembled the finest of silks you could imagine. A small perfect nose didn't distract you from her off-putting green eyes. An amazing Caribbean Sea green reflected in her irises. Her stunning looks could have her on any catwalk in the world or fashion magazine cover.

With Elia set to arrive soon, she would also see that, the trees, shrubs and flowers surrounding the property had gone wild with the abandonment. The roses needed to be trimmed as they now appeared messy and covered with dead dried buds. The grass was surrounded by numerous dried and tall overgrown weeds. It all needed tending in order to restore the grounds back to its original elegance. Next to the gate of the white picket fence that fronted the old Victorian, was a crusty brass plaque that read:

The House of Pearl
501 Bridgeway, Sausalito, California
Built in 1888
By Captain Edwin "The Pearl" Harrison

Chapter 3

Back at home now after this last triumphant concert, Elia thought of how tomorrow she would return to the grand old home in Sausalito. She had started to pack her belongings and found herself remembering the last time she had seen her parents alive.

The pain and loss of being alone throughout her youth and adult life, still stuck with her today. She had success but still she yearned to have had them with her longer, before their untimely death. Her inner pain was just as real now, as it was many years ago. She would never know what it would be like to have them now in her life, to have shared her successes and failures with them, or to just have another chance to sit and chat with them.

Time had enabled her to move on, but it did not allow her to forget.

As a child, Elia and her parents went on many day trips. Her father loved to discover new nature walks and places of interest and Elia's mom was a keen hobbyist with photography. She had even published some of her own nature photos in leading geographical magazines; therefore she was always up for another adventure with her husband and small daughter. Elia recalled taking photos with an instant camera, her mom would always give her on their trips. She always tried to imitate her mother. Both her parents were totally in love with each other, they had built a strong bond during their years together so Elia had a warm home environment that she remembered fondly.

Elia remembered one trip they took one winter, the snow was just beginning to fall down, fluttering lightly across the mountaintops, and the long roads leading to this place seemed to continuously wind on and on.

The winter chill had arrived. The flowers had turned into hibernating buds until spring returned to warm them again. The only plants little Elia watched streaming by the car window, were the pine trees and other evergreens that lined the forest for miles. She wondered what animals roamed wild within these trees. She wondered if she would see one. She hoped to see a bear.

A picnic basket was packed in the back seat where Elia sat and she could smell the chicken, salad, rolls, and freshly baked cookies. She recalled just wanting to eat them, even to sneak one out of the basket when her mom and dad were busy in a discussion about the most scenic roads to take. She could still smell that cookie smell to this day. It was the last peaceful aroma she could remember before the accident that took everything away from her. Even now, Elia would bake cookies just to feel closer to a time once lost and a time she longed to have more of.

Now late in the evening and taking a break from her packing, Elia poured herself another tea and remembered as a young girl how she searched eagerly through the green trees covered in light snowfall, for some kind of movement, for the leaves to move and there would be a wild animal! She searched for an animal to appear, to take the perfect photo to show her mom. Elia smiled to herself remembering the younger girl that she was then and she sat down and reminisced even more.

Elia remembered the cold air blowing in through her window when she rolled it down with vigor as it was stuck from the snow icing up outside its surface. She used both hands to wind it down some more and the air chilled her checks. Her mom quickly told her to close the window and Elia remembered rolling it back up fast, just to please her mom.

The road had few cars on it that day. Elia and her family had been driving several hours and the road looked black and dark from the wetness that the melted snow glazed over its surface. Elia could see other families driving by her window. Some were in RVs, others in cars packed fully in the back seat, with suitcases and thermal wear piled up on the seats pushing up against the windows. Some had rows of skis strapped to their car roofs and others had luggage covered with tarps over them. Many families were heading in this direction, to the snowcapped mountains, and it would be a while before they got to their location. The mountains always got busy this time of year as the school Ski Week break was on and Elia was happy to be on a new adventure with her mom and dad.

⚓

Elia finished her tea and looked at the crumpled photo she still had in her bag. It had creases all of over it and the color had faded from it, but she loved that photo. Elia had earned piles of money as a musician but this small photo meant more to her than anything else in the world. It was priceless!

Elia's mom and dad were chatting about where she could take some pretty pictures once they arrived at their location. Elia recalled them smiling and joking that day in the front seat. She remembered taking her camera out and setting it to take a candid shot from the middle of the back seat. She quickly snapped a photo of her mom and dad when they were in her viewfinder, while they both said *"Elia!"* She smiled at them and sat back in her seat excited she had captured them and she couldn't wait to process the film and see what it looked like.

At that time Elia did not know that, that photo would be the last photo of her parents taken or the last words her parents would say to her. She felt sad as she looked at this crumpled photo but she also felt happy as she knew how much they loved her.

The snow started to fall heavily and the windshield had piled up with icy residue. A storm was approaching and the cars began to drive slower. Elia's dad drove slower too. The road was now moving at a snail's pace. Then, the sudden sound of brakes screeching, crunching metal and glass breaking, and car horns blaring became an ongoing echo that seemed to last a long time, but in reality, it was only seconds. A large cargo truck that was taking food up the mountain had skidded across the icy road and cars swerved around as they honked their horns and moved out of its path. The truck driver had swerved away from hitting a deer but now his load was too heavy and he couldn't control the truck as it spun out on the icy road. The truck swerved around and pulled backwards and slid towards Elia's car. Elia's dad tried to move, however, cars had him sandwiched in from each side and he pulled the car over slightly out from the truck's way. Then the truck seemed to slide out of control towards Elia's car and in seconds, out of nowhere, it was flying towards her.

The windshield was shattered! The cold air raced in and the front of the car was locked up against the side of the now-stalled truck. The truck no longer moved. No car horns were going. Everything was silent! Being so young, Elia had no comprehension of what just happened. She looked at her arms and saw cuts from the windshield's glass and she could see her parents covered in blood and motionless. Other cars were trapped and smashed near her and the distant sirens of paramedics could be heard. Elia knew they were dead. She knew her parents were dead otherwise they would have moved to see if she was alive. She sat and stared at them hanging like lifeless puppets in front of her. The smell of freshly baked cookies was gone and she could only smell the pine trees and the smell of fear.

Paramedics arrived and she was lifted out of the vehicle by two men and taken to the local hospital. Elia said nothing as they tried to speak to her. What could she say? She was lost in her thoughts of fear, she knew her parents had died. She was alone. She was terrified!

The sound of the windscreen smashing and breaking, kept playing over in her mind as she was tended to at the hospital Emergency Room. She was afraid. Elia sat quietly as they fussed around her. She held tight onto the camera and would not let it go.

⚓

Elia washed her teacup and put away that photo that she loved. She remembered meeting Stanley. The man who would be her guardian, and who had taken care of her. She was fortunate she was not lost in the foster care system and that this man had come along. Stanley was an actor and he showed Elia a secure childhood, but she never stopped wanting her parents to come back and be alive and be a real family again.

Stanley was a compassionate man and proved to be what Elia needed as a child with no parents. Now Elia was a success and she was financially secure, but she missed her parents every day.

Elia tidied up what belongings she was taking to the house, a house that she had not seen in quite some time. That mournful day where her parents were killed in the car accident was something that she would never forget. Not only was it tragic, but she also reminisced on it fondly as it was the last time she spent with her mom and dad.

Elia remembered how her mom would pack their items for their road trips days in advance. Elia's mom was always organized and excited about the road trips they took together as a family. While Elia packed her own belongings now, she found herself folding her clothes in the same manner her mom would pack her clothes as a child, on their travels. She wondered if they would be proud of her success as a musician. Many times her mom and dad would play the piano and try and teach Elia a few tunes. Elia had packed her bags and she was excited to get to the house she had left so long ago, and to see what more she could find out about her family.

As she left the bustling lifestyle of a successful musician, Elia was not sad in any way to cast it aside. It was a time in her life where she wanted answers. Contrary to what she would be searching for, she had no idea what evil awaited her at that house. Elia wanted to know more about her family, her ancestors and her background. She wanted something to solidify any kind of information about her family that lived in that house, but would this house with its supernatural evil intentions allow her to find this peace?

The house stood there waiting for her arrival and soon Elia was to begin her own adventure, one totally unlike the adventures she spent with her mom and dad on those many road trips.

Elia couldn't believe that she even had the courage to go back to that house. She had spent many years running from it and now after she read that letter she knew this was what she had to do.

Elia's phone rang and it was Andrew.

"El, I've booked you a flight to leave first thing in the morning, but are you sure you want to take time off now, you're so hot now?" Andrew said sympathetically.

"We've been over this and I need to do this for myself," Elia told him with conviction.

"Okay Elia...I understand this is something you feel you need to do however, you have commitments to the label and you have commitments to your fans. I can tell it's something important to you, so deal with it and get back soon. I'll be here if you need anything."

"Thanks, Drew, and who knows, I may get inspiration for some new material. I shouldn't be there too long, and don't worry, I understand my commitments to the label."

"Elia I'll stay in touch with you and I'm sure you'll write some great new material. So everything is set for you. First class of course, straight to SFO, and the limo service will take you door to door."

"Thanks." Elia said and switched her phone off not to have any more interruptions. She just wanted to get to the house and do what she felt was now right for her.

Elia switched on the TV and drew herself a hot bath to relax before her journey back to a place that she had kept away from, purposely for many years. She poured some scented bath oils into the bath, lit several candles, and filled the bath to the bubbly brim. She wasn't too sure what state that old house would be in and she was determined to enjoy this bath tonight. The fragrant oils filled the air around her and the candles flickered in the large bathroom. Her Malibu beach home was huge and the open luxury of her master bathroom suite was something that she especially savored tonight, not knowing what was to come tomorrow.

When she awoke early the next morning, the sun was just coming up through a valley between the hills behind her Malibu Beach compound. Elia thought about the short flight that she was soon to take, and then as she looked out over the Pacific Ocean she thought about the beautiful California Coastline and she knew she felt up for the drive. Maybe to clear her head, maybe to smoke a joint, something she hadn't done in years, whatever it was, she now looked forward to the trip. It would take her 8 hours and it was a gorgeous warm day, so why not. She told herself that she would put the top down, blast some tunes, take her time and get some sun. Yes, the drive would do her good.

She texted Andrew, "Cancel flight, I'm driving up. Will keep my phone on. TTYL!"

She packed her bags quickly, grabbed her purse and her well worn guitar case. Then went to the garage and uncovered one of her prized possessions, a pristine, fully restored, 1965 Ford Galaxie 500 convertible. She loved this car and smiled at its strength and elegance: it was baby blue with supple crisp white leather interior and a sound system to rival the best of them. In this oversized garage her other, more modern, supercars would have to wait for her to return to get some of her attention.

"Hello sexy, up for a drive?" She threw her bags in the trunk, pulled her hair back in a sleek ponytail, tightened up her head scarf and climbed in and started the car. It started perfectly and the engine roared as if it were elated to have her in it.

Shades on, top down, Elia was on her way up the Pacific Coast Highway.

Chapter 4

She was right, the drive was amazing, she had forgotten how spectacular California was. Elia realized she had rushed out without eating, so she stopped at a roadside café in Oxnard for a quick breakfast before she got up onto Highway 101. She made amazing time, passing through Santa Barbara and San Luis Obispo without any trouble. She made it through Solvang without getting a ticket. Then passed by the huge cattle ranch near King City where she wished her top had been up because of the foul odor coming from thousands of cattle.

By now it was early afternoon as she drew nearer to San Francisco, Elia wondered if she would ever find that sense of family that she longed for from that old unnerving home. But for now, she relished in the sights, smells, and the crisp cool clean air of the San Francisco Bay Area.

As she drove north over the Golden Gate Bridge, Elia took the "Sausalito Exit" and drove through the golden covered hills: her canvas top was down and the wind blew a strand of her dark hair that had escaped from her tightly fitting scarf. She slowed down and rounded a turn and saw the houses of Sausalito climbing up the hills. Her hit song was playing on the radio, but it didn't matter, she still felt a little trepidation knowing she was almost back at that House of Pearl.

As she drove through Sausalito, memories began to flood her head, then she saw it, the house, sitting like some sentinel on the waterfront of Sausalito. Beckoning too her. Anyone who didn't know might think it was a picture-perfect house, but Elia knew better. Beyond the white picket fence and the big bay windows looking out towards the big city across the bay, a strange occurrence seemed to be shadowing a secret within its quiet rooms.

Meanwhile, a cracked stained glass window on the lower level of this two-story home, missing a few small pieces of its intricate design, possibly forgotten about many years ago, acted like a whistle while the weathering salty bay air blew through it. Just above the window, the weathered paint blew off in strips and swirled up and away from the old house.

For a hundred and twenty years the unpredictable bay winds gusted off the churning bay water. Now they whistled through the old window trying to warn anybody of the danger within, when a white, ghostly figure seemed to try and stretch out through the missing pieces of glass. The window remained rigidly in place, but the figure floated freely about. Ghostlike, the eerie figure moved in a swaying motion out of the home, into the air, and then quickly raced back inside the house while wailing loudly through the stained glass window. Was this an illusion caused by the peeling paint and strong misty bay breezes hitting and swirling around the big old house? Or was something more paranormal still possessing this home?

Still, no one other than the local sea birds or the lone lost tourist who ignored her small child who pulled on her skirt and tried to show her what he had seen, was nearby enough to see this strange occurrence. In one quick moment, on the creaky steps of the porch another ghostly figure appeared and vanished just as quickly as if knowing someone was coming.

A muffled thump of her music disrupted the surrounding air as she steadily approached the house. The music on the radio was still her latest hit single. Lost in the rhythm, Elia's mind bounced from one thought to another for new songs she planned to record.

As for the house, she knew this wasn't a simple inheritance, she remembered the troubles she and her grandmother had with the house twenty years earlier. She knew this was going to be touchy, but also great inspiration for some great new songs.

The howling whistle that seemed to embrace the house settled quietly as it sensed Elia's approach. The tarnished front door knob creaked and opened up as Elia gently pushed her way inside. Elia, with her guitar case and a large Louis Vuitton bag over her shoulder, and a small duffle bag in her other hand, took a slow inventory, as she stood open-mouthed in the entrance hall. Dust was everywhere and cobwebs filled almost every corner. Energized by her drive up the coast she got right to work as she cleaned up the old home to make it livable.

The sounds of her boots were heard squeaking on the polished maple floorboards as she walked through the home and cleaned up. The old wooden ladder was still in the hallway set up like it was yesterday. Set up to climb into the attic. She looked up into the dark hole in the ceiling remembering what had happened up there so many years ago.

She knew what an unusually beautiful evening it was going to be, she decided to climb the dusty old wooden ladder and bring some things with her. She took what she needed from the overnight bag and dropped a bottle of Chardonnay into her oversized purse. She climbed the ladder carefully. She passed through the large attic, now emptied of its gruesome contents, and then just that quickly, she had a tingling of the old fear, why?

Eventually she climbed out onto the roof top deck through

a large open hatch. With her she had her guitar, and in her bag she had some old sheets of music and a bottle of wine. She was surprised to find a little folding chair on the "Widow's Walk" as it was commonly called when it was built by Captain Harrison so long ago. She sat down and absorbed the view of her inheritance and the surrounding landscape below. It was a still, warm evening and it was so clear that the stars twinkled, perfect for viewing the most beautiful city in the world.

Once she got comfortable, she pulled out her cell phone and checked it for tweets, text messages, and then emails. Her old acoustic guitar that she carried everywhere was lying next to her. She sat in the little chair and she sighed as she smiled at the million-dollar scenic view that surrounded her.

The San Francisco skyline was lighting up now, boats anchored for the night just off shore, the Bay Bridge, Angel Island, Alcatraz and the rising moon were all visible this evening and set ablaze by the twinkling lights of the City. It was a landscape that many have painted and photographed over the years, but to see it on this night was something else, something magical. Elia confirmed this as she looked from side to side to capture the whole experience. This sight was spectacular! It was a vast twilight view of the city with a rising moon that came up between Angel Island and the San Francisco skyline. The moon was so large that Elia felt that she could reach out and touch it.

The moon glistened romantically and the air was sweet smelling from the night jasmine hedge next door. This would be a perfect evening for a date with a man that she loved or lusted for. But, for now she sat alone and the home was quiet and she had no idea about the body lying below it or the paranormal occurrences that were still happening around her. She thought that was over, and that all the spirits were long gone, but she would soon find out that they never left.

Each light that glistened shone in a multitude of colors,

reds, blues, yellows and whites. San Francisco was lit to impress everyone tonight! The City glittered and glowed in its magnificence as a "Hornblower" dinner boat cruised by. The three-story yacht was alive and exploding with a large social party of over four hundred guests. The boat had navy blue hulls and bright white decks and it glided like an elegant swan on the still bay water. The guests seemed attractive and well-dressed as laughter and music surrounded its gliding motions. The tapping of glasses for toasts with applause could be heard throughout the harbor.

Elia soaked in the view with intrigue and wondered how nice it would be to be out there now. But she sat back and enjoyed her first night back at the House of Pearl. Maybe she would find more family connections and maybe here she could write some new music, or maybe she really just needed a break from her busy music career and the people who glommed onto her because she was famous, and very rich. It seemed the home was behaving so far, and for her first night nothing would deter her. The oversized Tabby cat rubbed up against Elia's leg and began to purr a warning to her, but tonight, she relaxed with her wine and watched San Francisco twinkle like Wonderland.

Several days had passed and Elia had begun to clean up the place as best she could. Not wanting to sleep in the back rooms, she chose to sleep on the raised bed in the dining room. It was during this process, she thought she saw various unusual and unexplainable occurrences around her, she felt a little strung out by it and promptly answered the call coming in from Andrew.

"You know, umm, I just don't know if I'm ready. I mean the demo is done. I just don't think I can keep doing this anymore, Andrew. I just need some time off and this old spooky house might be the answer for a well-earned break from touring and recording."

"Elia, take a break, even hide-away in that old house, but that can't stop you from being in the public eye, and besides my talented friend, you should take time out for fun, you're way too intense." Andrew lectured.

"This house is great, but..."

"But what? You've only been there a couple of days, what's wrong?" Andrew asked with interest, she happened to be his most famous client and he had a major vested interest in her.

"This house is so strange, but for some reason, I sleep really well here. My Grandmother and I cleaned this place out of any ghosts all those years ago. But sometimes over the last few days I've seen figures out of the sides of my eye, moving by, like a ghost, then I look back and there's nothing... ha-ha, you probably think I'm crazy now."

"That's very funny, but no, I don't think that, El. Maybe you should go to a nearby hotel. I don't know if I like this, my brightest star alone in a place that sounds old and creepy. I don't want anything to happen to you. I suppose if you get overly freaked out, it could be fodder for creativity, you need to stay calm, think lyrics and get ready for the next album."

"Always my agent, Andrew, no, no I'll be fine, it's probably nothing, it's probably because I'm here alone."

"Well creepy or not, it sounds silly to stay if you're not comfortable. Or maybe a man could be what you need there, how long has it been?"

"Andrew really! You know what; getting laid is not high on my list of priorities right now." Elia started rolling her eyes, but she knew he really cared for her a great deal.

"What? And here I thought I had a sex goddess for a client, ha-ha, you know, with all your love song hits, it should always be high on your list, Sweetie."

"If the only thing on your mind is my personal sex life then you seriously need to GET A LIFE!" Elia stated, slightly agitated by Andrew's remark knowing full well that he meant no harm.

"Elia, sweetie, I just care, that's all. So you're sure you're fine with staying there?"

"Yeah, forget I said anything."

"Sure El, how's your music really coming along?"

"Andrew, I'm playing with some ideas. Next time we'll talk more about my illustrious singing career. Love you oodles, bye!" She blew a kiss into the phone sarcastically.

Perched on her rooftop spot again, Elia switched off the phone and dropped it onto the tray that was next to her. The tray held a bottle of chardonnay and a glass half full. Next to the tray was an iPod with iTunes cued up, and some yellowed and stained old papers she had brought up with her. The old blemished papers had music and lyrics written on them. These papers seemed very old, and had been forgotten and lost for a long, long time. The hand written compositions were in a fancy calligraphy with the name of Prima Pearl as the author. Who was she? This material obviously interested Elia.

She picked up the glass of wine and took a healthy gulp from it and toasted it to her party of one.

She leaned over and touched the play button on the iPod, picked up her old guitar and started playing along. She was a little buzzed and enjoyed her private party of one overlooking the magnificent bay. The wine had taken its affect and Elia forgot about the strange occurrences she had experienced in the previous few days and continued to play her guitar for anyone to hear.

A beautiful one hundred and twenty foot luxury sailboat had come in to the harbor and was dropping its anchor. This elegant boat was just a couple hundred feet from the front of Elia's old Victorian home and she looked down at it and smiled at its elegance.

This boat was a technological masterpiece! The interior was spacious and elegantly appointed with exotic woods and fine fabrics. The wood was dark brown and lacquered up with a bright shine. The brass and chrome fittings were polished state-of-the-art hardware, and it was a well-tended elegant ship, its deck seemed to go on forever and it could easily be big enough for a family and crew to live on.

Today the boat had been taken for a short bay cruise after a long voyage around the Pacific Ocean with its owners and crew of four experienced sailors. The owner's daughter, Renee, was a wild teenager and on this evening her parents were below resting, and Renee took full advantage of their absence. She was trying out a new halter-top that left nearly nothing to the imagination, given its size and form fitting fabric; obviously she loved to show off her young, sexy figure.

She was young, wealthy and beautiful, and she knew it. Her tight, hip-hugging white denim shorts revealed just enough of her derriere to be sexy beyond her years. She very unexpectedly came out of the main salon and climbed up onto the fly bridge.

At the helm of the boat closing things up for the night was Paul Hamilton, a fit muscular man. With sun-streaked brown hair, he was tall, tanned and a licensed professional boat handler and captain. His looks were what you'd expect to find if you had dreamed of a blue-eyed, striking, sea-faring man. He was skippering this ship and he was very qualified and capable of the job at hand. He was in his thirties, and had worked for the owners of the boat for many years and was a fine captain. He was a single ladies' man, and that fact had never interfered with his ability to captain any ship, that was, up until Renee, who recently turned eighteen. Her blooming sexuality had not really been problematic for him, even so, he still indulged in a bit of flirtation with her, after all he thought, it can't hurt. *Right*?

Renee flirtatiously sauntered up to him, while he was lashing down various loose items. Then she pretended to work the rigging as if it were a stripper pole. She was more than aware of her youth and sexuality, and this did not go unnoticed by Paul. He tried to be coy as he secured the anchor and lowered the second anchor line until it hit the bay mud and locked up.

"Hey Paul, watcha doin'?" Renee said flirtatiously.

With her following him around the deck like a puppy, they returned to the fly bridge.

"You know Renee, your mom and dad are down below, and that brother of yours is always sneaking around, so I would watch it with your little games, OK?" Paul said, trying to be authoritative, but as he said it, he couldn't help but look at her up and down, *"man; she's grown up this last year" he thought to himself.*

Renee was not a girl to take "no" for an answer, and she continued to follow Paul around on deck like a love-struck teen.

Below, the voices of the owners of the boat could be heard, Charles and Lydia West, were up and about on the second salon level with two of their other children on board with them. A boy, Joshua, sixteen and a girl, Katy, aged six are below deck with them.

Lydia yelled from below, "Renee, leave Paul alone, you've got homework to do, young lady, and you're behind enough as it is. And dinner's almost ready, come down and help me set the table."

Renee shrugged her shoulders, and smiled, and sashayed away.

After securing the yacht, Paul picked up a bag and pulled out a sketchpad. He found a secluded spot on the bow and sat down. While he sketched the city skyline, Paul couldn't help hearing a trail of music coming from behind him on the Sausalito shoreline. When he looked up at the source, he could sort of make out a character on the roof of the old Victorian. He thought he might have seen her before, but wasn't sure.

After a short while, Renee came back to the deck to find that Paul was not sketching but was listening intently to the music, as if he were bewitched. She leaned over towards him, but he didn't notice her presence, he was transfixed on something onshore.

Renee got a twinge of jealousy.

"Umm, dinner." Renee said to Paul, flirtatiously; but he was transfixed by the singing.

"Paul? Hello. What's up? Have you even noticed I have been talking to you?"

"No."

Renee was irritated.

"I mean yes, sorry, what's up?" Paul replied.

"You didn't even notice it."

"Of course I noticed you, it's pretty hard not to."

"No, I mean, look, what do you think of it?" Renee said.

Paul was tired of this game.

"Fine, let's see, turn around, no... same old perfect teenage butt. Your hair isn't any different. Wait a minute, turn back around, yep that's it; you pierced your belly button. How did I miss that?"

"Hot, right? I've kept it covered, I did it in Hawaii right before we left, and it's just now looking good, after the healing and everything. It was kinda nasty at first."

She moved closer to him, so that he could see it better.

Paul looked around with concern, "Are your parents nearby? Are you trying to get me fired?"

"No, I just thought that, we're going to be here awhile, so maybe you and I could chill and hang a little, maybe go up to the top of that mountain."

"That's Mount Tamalpais, the 'Sleeping Maiden,' which is what you should be doing soon. Renee, come, sit here."

"On your lap?"

"Yea, come on. I'll tell you a little secret."

Renee looked pensive, but excited, she came closer to him and she slowly slipped onto his lap.

"Like this?"

"That's nice, look at me, what do you see?"

"A kind, rugged, older guy, who wants me, but won't admit it to himself."

Renee boldly leaned in to kiss Paul, but he was distracted at the last second just before her lips touched his. Elia's music penetrated the air. He was a womanizer without any regard to how many women he seduced, and he didn't seem to care much about what he did to them, he just fell in lust first and maybe allowed questions after.

He listened to her music, lifted Renee off of his lap, got up and walked away from her towards the Boston Whaler.

"So honey, tell your parents I'm going over to Horizon's for a while…. Do you hear that? I think there's someone singing on that roof, I might know them? Doesn't that sound like you've heard it before?"

"It's that hit song I was playing yesterday, you jerk! I hate you! You're so lame!" She stood there indignantly, hands on her hips, mad at his rejection.

Paul jumped into the sixteen-foot Boston Whaler and looked back at Renee. The boat was one that's used as a ship-to-shore boat when not in use for water skiing. He pushed off, revved the engine, blew Renee a kiss and sped off, leaving a froth of white water in his absence.

Paul could be heard yelling out, "I love you honey, really."

Renee looked after him and flipped him her middle finger. *"Asshole."*

Chapter 5

*T*he evening was glorious and unusually warm. Elia sat and continued to sing and write as she strummed her guitar with passion for her art. She was entranced in her own song, and was singing a particular song that her grandmother had written that she had adapted into a big hit. She liked the lyrics of this family song, however, she had adapted it to her own style of ballad. Elia sang as light night breezes blew around Sausalito and she watched the partygoers' boats as they tied off at the bar's private docks.

Cars pulled up to the valet at the Horizon Restaurant and other dockside clubs while boats tied up to its courtesy guest dock. Porsches, Benz, clunkers and trucks, and other luxury models all occupied the same lot. There was a mish-mash of age groups that flowed in and out of the bar. The eclectic mix included everyone from young partygoers to older well-heeled folks. The most popular bar seemed to be Horizons, a staple of Sausalito party life for years. Horizons, was also a great bar and occupied a turn-of-the-century landmark building. The venerable old white building was built in 1898, and once housed the San Francisco Yacht Club. It was definitely the place to be seen in Sausalito. Horizons, has hosted yacht races, regattas, and gala parties for almost a hundred years.

Back in the 1960's when it was last remodeled inside, it was called the "Trident" a party hangout for celebrities and rockers alike; everyone from The Stones, Jimi Hendrix, Joan Baez, Bob Dylan, The Byrds and Janis Joplin. A lot of drugs and drinking and sex went on in there over the years, much more then, than now, but it still attracted a heavy drinking crowd from all over the Bay Area as well as the world.

As the evening went on, Elia, from her rooftop perch, watched the lives of the others below. She could hear faint laughter and music. This made her introspective and she began to feel lonely on her rooftop perch. When she saw a loving couple come out hand in hand, then embrace against their car, before getting in and leaving, it zeroed in on her empty heart. She wondered deeply about the importance of her career, and now again that home that she had inherited, and how nice it would have been to have someone beside her tonight, but as usual, it was her and her alone, alone with her old guitar, the ghosts of her family and this empty old house.

Elia wondered what her life would be like if her parents hadn't died when she was a little girl. She surely would have been down at the restaurant with the others, a life much less lonely. She might have had two or three children by now and a devoted husband. Mom and Dad would come visit on the weekends while she and her husband and their family sailed off to exotic destinations and languished in their love and happy life. Elia wove a lovely life quilt in her head.

Back to reality, Elia looked around shaking off the memories of her lonely childhood and the death of her parents, and being abandoned by her grandmother. Trying to distract herself, she looked at the action below; she then spotted the athletic Paul. He was tying his boat to the dock before beginning his search for a good time at Horizons.

Elia was watching him as she sang away. Sensing Elia in some strange way, he turned and looked up directly at her. He had liked the music when he heard it with Renee, however, now it was closer and he felt pulled into her lyrics. He liked everything about it. It actually felt familiar to him. For some time, he had been mesmerized by her music mixed with the beauty of the night. Elia noticed the directness of his gaze as he watched her and listened. She suddenly felt very self-conscious, and quickly retreated from the moonlight back into the darkness of the house.

After packing her music away, she headed for the kitchen. She leaned over the counter and prompted her iPad to play softly in the background. While she slowly sipped more wine, Elia let her thoughts return to the man she had seen staring back at her.

Paul shook his head, as this trance-like spell was broken. As the music stopped, he noticed Elia had vanished. He could have listened to her all night long. He turned around to face the nightlife, while promising himself that he should concentrate on the business at hand... a stiff drink and some female company. In his mind, what else was there? He strolled in as if it were his second home. Honestly it was... he was always at this bar when he was in Sausalito.

"Russian Standard... on the rocks, beautiful, thanks" Paul smiled as he ordered from the new curvaceous bartender.

As he drank his vodka, Paul's eyes caught something, a twin pair of twenty-something blondes at the other end of the bar. They were scantily dressed and were obviously looking for action this night with their toned and tanned bodies, which they had no reservations flaunting. Paul smiled at them as he lifted his drink to his lips. Both twins liked what they saw and eagerly approached him.

"Ladies," he said confidently.

"Hey there," they giggled and at the same time smiled in unison.

Paul gulped the last of his cocktail before slamming it down on the bar and winked at the bartender. He watched the shapely blondes glide over to where he sat. The girls put their matching, metal-clad Versace bags on the bar on either side of Paul that created a human sandwich. The hot bartender laid out three shot glasses and poured ice chilled Russian Standard into three shot glasses and winked back at Paul. "Enjoy."

As he tried to be playful and begin a conversation, Paul asked, "So, which one of you two is the older one?" in a half-teasing effort to get the conversation rolling.

"She is, but I'm the nastier one. I'm Sandy," Sandy said confidently.

"Well I guess time will tell, won't it Sandy? What's *your* name?" Paul flashed a George Clooney smile to the other twin.

"I'm Candy."

"Of course you are," Paul smiled with charm. "I'm Paul, Paul Hamilton."

"So what can we get for you Paul Hamilton?" Candy asked while she stroked his arm sensually.

"I'm torn between a "Sex on a Beach" or a "Stroke at Midnight" he said devilishly. He handed them each their shot of vodka. "But start with this."

The girls laughed at his obvious innuendo and threw back their chilled shots. "That's funny because I think we can help you out with that. We've got this little compound out at Stinson Beach. It has an amazing sound system and a big, big private beach."

"I'm all about taking in the local sights, girls. Let's go."

Before another drink could be ordered or before the ice would begin to melt; the three of them were off for a wild night of sensuality. Paul thought to himself, sometimes I just can't help myself. *I really am an asshole, but I do love the ladies....*

Far from the thrilling sex party Paul was having, Elia, in her flannel jammies with her iPod earplugs in, had been cleaning up in the kitchen with her bunny slippers after having finished far too many glasses of wine by herself during the course of the night. She swayed to and fro in her fluffy flannels as she cleaned, and danced to a tune in her head. The imagined tune seemed to be from another time or place. It had her moving, side to side, sensually, as if she were dancing with a real partner, rather than a figment of her imagination. As she lost herself in the tune she whispered.

"Edwin. Oh my love…"

Who was Edwin? Was she possessed? Or was she just too drunk to even know where she was? Strangely, a music box began to play in the corner of the old kitchen. With no one spinning its lever, the intricate workings of the tiny ensemble moved in perfect unison by themselves. The old Japanese music box, inlaid with pearls and gems, seemed to automatically select an ancient melody. Sweet and sad, it had a strong, hypnotizing effect on Elia.

Strangely, Elia seemed to be a completely different person as the music box played. Her face was reflecting the face of another woman. The loneliness buried deep within Elia became a distant memory as the mysterious entity embodied her. The buttons on her flannel top popped loose revealing her ample breasts which she began to massage.

The paranormal occurrences had become more frequent now, and seemed to have taken control of Elia's innocence. Though her partner remained invisible, Elia seemed to be happily dancing with a very loving man… a man that was a mere shadow in her arms. Elia's eyes were closed as she tilted her head onto the imaginary shoulder of her partner. Blissfully, they moved together as if they were lovers. She lifted herself up onto the counter with her legs spread as if her lover was consuming her sexuality.

Oddly enough, being used by the paranormal forces within this home was not unknown to her. Many years earlier, with her grandmother, she had extricated the house of two ghosts. Now, the beginning of an onslaught of odd happenings had started, unbeknownst to poor Elia, the events of this night had begun stories that should have remained sealed forever. Elia danced as a medium for another soul, and was lost in this crazy occurrence of a phantom love affair, and in these moments, her loneliness had vanished temporarily.

The strange night had now passed, and another day in Sausalito was dawning. The early morning fishermen had taken up their spots across the street on the bay's edge, and Sausalito's many shops were opening their doors for another day's business. This day dawned with new possibilities or a chance that Elia might leave this old house. Or perhaps she wouldn't. Perhaps she was destined to be there. Maybe there was a purpose for her presence. Her destiny or her demise: only time would tell.

Elia was suffering a horrid hangover and was not pleased with herself-to say the least. She was confused how she woke up with her flannel top opened up and bunched under her arms.

As she rolled over one more time high up on the stilted bed, she reached for more painkillers, the thought of the chores on her list just made her pain worse. She moved ever so slowly, she relaxed on the large raised bed and just stared out the window. Lost in thought for a moment, she imagined herself moving closer to someone she wanted to make love to, but as she stroked her hand along the mattress, she found only emptiness. She rolled her eyes and dismissed her silly thoughts as just an alcohol-induced misfiring in her subconscious and she slowly rose to meet the day.

She carefully lowered herself down from the bed, buttoned up her flannel top, put on her slippers and walked into the kitchen holding her head, hoping for relief from her hangover, and readied herself to begin her chores for the day.

She methodically dropped her flannel jammies and jumped into the shower. Afterwards she pulled up her stretch-tight blue jeans and a loose-fitting, white pullover V-neck sweater, it was simple yet sexy. Elia quickly slid her feet into a pair of black J. Crew flip-flops; her toes were perfectly manicured with her brightly painted red nails on full display. Grabbing her keys and her purse, she skipped her way outside and down the wide wooden staircase and through the white picket fences gate.

She shook her hair out, hoping that if she looked good, she would feel better.

Right there in front of her house, was her Galaxie convertible. She smiled at her vintage muscle car. She folded down the canvas top and secured it. Then she climbed in and stroked the soft white leather interior. The old car started right away as usual, and the low rumble of the old V-8 tickled the windows of the houses and shook the flowerbeds, sending a cluster of bees skyward. Then she pulled a U-turn and drove towards town.

The weather was perfect for her top down drive through town to "Mollie Stone's" grocery store. She drove through downtown Sausalito passing by the early-bird tourists and saw the endless marinas surging with yachts and sailboats on her right. After she got to the grocery store, Elia noticed that the store was very busy so she wrapped herself up with a headscarf and large sunglasses. She went up and down the aisles and collected an assortment of fine foods for home. After all... she did love to cook.

She felt secure with her oversized sunglasses and scarf, sure no one would recognize her. But the store was filled with old wealthy women, most of whom surely didn't know who she was anyway, or more than likely didn't care. In this town, old money wouldn't be impressed with a pop star. Elia relaxed a bit with this realization.

The store was small, but stocked with gourmet items, from fresh-fare gourmet meals to organic produce; it was a small high-end grocery store, not your average neighborhood mini-mart. She bought some extra muffins for a morning snack, then returned to her car and loaded the bags into her trunk. She was ready to head back home, but as Elia turned the key, the car didn't start.

"What the hell? C'mon, start up," as she pounded on the steering wheel, she was not pleased with the car. "You never stall."

Elia looked around somewhat frantically as some of her groceries needed refrigeration. She noticed a face she thought looked familiar. It was the man who was staring up at her last night as she was singing. It was Paul, standing on the gas docks filling up his Boston Whaler. Unaware she had seen him, Paul continued to chat and exchange party stories with the gas jockey, Griff, and a young squirrelly kid, Nicky.

"Dude, the twins? No way!" said Griff, the young, heavily tattooed gas dock attendant.

"Bro, they're soooo hot!" Nicky added in a surfer-esque accent.

"What can I tell you, gentleman? I just got 'it,' you know what I'm sayin'?" Paul bragged.

"Their dad is like a gazzillionaire. He owns like, half of Silicon Valley or something like that, dude."

"And all I got was a good time and sore back.... Damn," Paul laughed. The others guys laughed too, although with a little bit of jealousy.

Elia tried over and over to start the car, but got nothing. So she readjusted her sunglasses and tightened up her pale yellow scarf to try and hide her identity, pulled up her jeans and reluctantly approached the laughing guys at the pumps.

"Uh, excuse me. Can any of you guys help me? My car won't start," she asked.

"Uh, well," Griff stumbled.

"Yeah, sure, what's wrong?" Paul said, taking charge of the situation.

"Hell, I don't know, it just won't start, it never does this."

Paul immediately recognized a hung-over woman, and jumped back onto the small boat, grabbed the keys and a canvas tool bag. Hopping back onto the dock, he threw the keys at Griff and slung the bag over his shoulder. "Hey watch this for me. If I'm not back by five, lock it up will you?" The gas dock guys shook their heads in idiotic agreement.

"He gets all the women doesn't he?" Griff looked proud of Paul.

"Lucky bastard, right Bro..." Nick responded in agreement. They both shook their heads at Paul's special chemistry with women as they watched him walk off with Elia. Her skin-tight jeans fit her shape perfectly, as her caboose swayed to and fro and confirmed their envy.

"We'll get you fixed up right away Miss, OK?" Paul assured her as he smiled back at her.

"Thanks," she said tentatively.

Paul was impressed with the Galaxie, as he looked it up and down, back and forth.

After a whistle usually reserved for a beautiful woman "This is a lotta muscle for a little lady."

"I can handle it," Elia said indignantly.

"I didn't mean anything by it... say, are you that famous singer... Elia?"

"I'm sorry, yes, I'm Elia, nice to meet you."

"Paul. Paul Hamilton." He reached out to shake her hand. As

they touched, they lingered just a second too long which made Elia uncomfortable. Not incredibly uncomfortable, but enough to make her blush like a young girl. Paul seemed taken aback by the obvious chemistry between them. He was used to one night stands... no emotions. Pop star or heiress it didn't matter to him. He obviously avoided emotions; they weren't conducive to his non-committal lifestyle choices. Paul thought, *she looks hot, I wonder if she's good in bed.*

"Alrightee, let's see what's going on. Pop the hood, will you, Elia?"

"Sure." She followed Paul's instruction and got in the car to open the hood. Under the hood of the Galaxie, Elia watched Paul as he fiddled with something here, something there, as she admired his confidence, handsome face and well-toned body.

"OK, start her up."

A turn of the key and the car started up right away. "You are a lifesaver. I really appreciate this," Elia said, Paul smiled back again and lowered the hood until it snapped shut. By now, he was covered in grease. With no towel in sight, he wiped his hands on his jeans, and made them dirty as well. Elia looked at him and laughed. They both laughed. "Do you want to come up to the house?" She asked tentatively, "You can wash up... and I'll cook you something for helping me."

Simultaneously, they both got into the car. With Elia at the wheel, she threw the car into drive and peeled out of the parking lot. Paul gripped the door handle for dear life. Elia's laughter echoed along the docks as they sped off.

Chapter 6

$\mathcal{T}$he dryer was grinding away on its high-cycle in the laundry room next to the kitchen. There was something hypnotic in the steady hum the machine made. With a pre-made quiche from the deli that was warming in the oven, and with the laundry going, Elia finally had a moment to actually examine her kitchen. Curiously, the décor was a mish-mash of cabinet styles, some Victorian and some from the 60's. Eclectic and visually messy, the house was badly in need of updating.

Paul was quietly standing at the opening to the kitchen with a towel that he had wrapped around his waist. He watched Elia. She couldn't help but notice his washboard abs, a result of years at sea and surfing, and his tanned muscular build, not to mention how good-looking he was. She was very attracted to him; he smiled back at her and sensed their mutual attraction.

A morning of simple chatting had led Elia into the kitchen to cook an impromptu mimosa brunch for this sexy guy who was now sitting at the table in her kitchen. Paul held the bottle low near his waist and he watched her with lust in his eyes as he popped the champagne bottle and watched it froth over the sides of the bottle being caught by the dish towel wrapped around it.

"I should go around fixing women's cars more often," Paul stated humorously.

"Oh yes. Who knows what other meals you'll score," Elia said jokingly as she checked the oven. She sipped her mimosa and smiled approvingly at her creation. She decided to make some homemade garlic bread, with thick chunks of Parmesan cheese that she tasted as she sprinkled it on the soft warm French bread.

Paul walked around the kitchen intrigued by the aromas coming from her cooking. He quietly watched Elia and it seemed she just got better looking with each glance and he felt drawn to her. He thought to himself, *"Am I just horny, or is this the real thing?"*

"Tell me, who's your interior designer? You really should take some photos of this and submit it to 'Architectural Creepers' magazine. You're a shoo-in for the cover."

"That's so not fair; I've only been here a few days. I'm also kinda creeped out by the place... my great grandparents died in that back bedroom."

"Seriously? I didn't know, I'm sorry."

"No worries, you hungry?" She shook it off, and wondered why she blurted that out.

"Oh yeah, I'm famished, and that smells so good, I can't say no. Can I help?"

She looked at his bare chest, and while his shirt was still drying, she realized that he was watching her too, "Uh, no, I'm good how about a refill on that Mimosa?"

"Now you're talking my language."

After Paul prepared her another Mimosa, he moved in closer to hand her the glass. She could smell his washed hair from the shampoo in her shower and she uncontrollably blurted out.

"You smell good."

"Thanks, I used some of your bath stuff."

There was a moment of stillness between them. He knew from his experience with women, she desired him and she's just trying to control that desire. Paul smiled and as he leaned over to sneak a piece of the garlic bread, he brushed his hand across her small waist and Elia leaned in closer to smell his chest and then he moved back from tasting it and their faces came close together. A kiss locked them together and they embraced with desire, as they kissed with passion. Elia had never felt anything like this before; she was so drawn to the man. She hardly knew this guy. Or did she know him? She felt like she did know him. It was all very confusing for her.

Her body was entwined with his; she was lost in this moment and didn't care why she was this free with a stranger. But it seemed to begin again, this veil of another woman within her was aroused and she was not just Elia, she was this other woman too, like the previous evening.

Elia touched Paul and prodded him to take the lead with her and he felt her passion, he also felt her prompting and reciprocated with a sensual caressing of her back and neck. As his face moved closer to hers he saw something was different about her.

"Elia, are you alright?" She didn't answer: she needed his sexuality.

A noise began to get louder as if it was the house creaking: Elia heard it.

"Did you hear that Paul?"

"Shush baby, I didn't hear anything..." He grabbed her hair and pulled her head into his neck as she kissed his neck passionately, then he kissed her back, and as they embraced, they fell back against the wall and small flickers of electricity flew out of the wall sockets and touched both of them, as if it were pursuing them, to connect to them. As the electrical plasma touched both of them, their kisses become more feverish and Paul grabbed Elia again and pulled her sweater over her head with a single masterful stroke and kissed her braless chest with eager desire. They were embroiled in their sensual desire and lost in its passion.

The old white plaster ceiling above them began to swirl like an upside down whirlpool. In the center a pearl shaped droplet began to form. It plummeted down from the high ceiling and landed on Paul's neck, and was quickly absorbed by his skin as it hit him; it emanated a pearl-like wash over his exposed body. He looked at Elia more longingly. This house was thriving on the fact that these two were together here and now, it was as if the house had planned it all along.

"Pearl... oh my precious Pearl..." Paul whispered, and was surprised to hear a tone in his voice he had never used with a woman before.

Deep in this trance of passion that consumed him, Paul pushed Elia up against the kitchen door with a bang, and slammed it shut in the process. She pushed him off and stood there and lowered her hands from her breasts and unsnapped her jeans then she smiled up at him; she too looked like someone else. Paul kissed her again even more passionately, while she loosened his towel. He picked her up and sat her on the edge of the kitchen counter and made mad passionate love to her. It was as if the two were a different man and woman making love; their passion for each other was intense and otherworldly.

The rest of the day and night was like a blur for Elia and Paul. They made love for hours, slept, and made love again, it was as if someone had put a spell on them and time seemed to stand still. They were in another world of passion and hunger for each other that lasted through the night, until they both passed out into deep satiated sleep.

The passion of the night was over as the new day began. Paul looked at Elia as she awakened; sunshine streamed in across the sheets.

"Hey," he whispered.

"Hey," was her sleepy reply.

"That was so intense... I mean amazing... wow, I've never, ever felt like this...." Paul said and he smiled toward Elia. She was totally shocked at what he had just said. After all, he must have had so many women in his life traveling the world, was this really that special for him? She forced herself to subdue her skepticism.

"Yeah, it's totally new for me too," Elia said as she lightly kissed his lips.

"You know, I've got some shore leave I'd like to use and I thought I'd stick around a bit today, since I noticed this place has a lot of things that need to be fixed. Like that leaky pipe in the bathroom and some of these old crooked doors are easy to fix. I can help if you like. Whaddya say?"

"Oh, that'd be great Paul, thanks, but don't think that you have to because we—"

"How about a tour of the house first?" Paul interrupted.

Elia smiled at Paul as they kissed again and casually made their way around the house for a tour.

"So why are so many of these doors locked, it's kinda weird, you know?" Paul asked as they walked though the house.

Elia thought long and hard, but answered honestly, well, when I was a kid, strange things happened all the time here, ghosts, sightings, things moving around without explanation. My grandmother had always wanted to do a séance to get rid of them; so she finally did and brought a psychic here, but that's another story for another day." Elia said as if she was used to them by now.

Now that she was back here in the house, she felt the same uneasiness she felt as a child before the exorcism. Elia thought for a moment, "I don't know, maybe in a way it's less lonely with the ghosts here, you know what I mean?"

"No, I don't know what you mean... and that's just plain creepy,

Elia." Paul said as he looked over his shoulder and half expected to see an apparition descend upon him.

But nothing was there. Paul heaved a sigh of relief.

"These old homes always have strange stories surrounding them. Tell me more about it," Paul inquired.

Eating their brunch together out on the front porch, Elia and Paul chatted about the house.

"I don't know what it is about this place, Elia, but it really does something to me. It makes me feel different, like I belong here. Maybe it's creepy, but it's so, alive." The stained-glass window below them whistled its ghostly sound. "You know what I mean?" Paul struggled to find the words to express how he felt.

"Oh yeah, I know."

"Usually, I couldn't care less where I am... or who I'm with. But it's different with you Elia, and I just don't get it." Paul seemed surprised by his own sincerity and openness.

"I know, the only person I'm attached to currently is my agent, and he's my gay boyfriend, my GBF, so maybe that doesn't even count, right?" Elia said, she smiled and was pleased to hear Paul's words.

"I guess you may have figured the same about me. Most women think I'm kind of an asshole. I don't tend to stick around." As Paul said this, he thought about all the women he had used over the years, women he never cared about. They always wanted him; one even asked him to marry her. But he ran off with her best friend and broke her heart. He didn't think twice about her.

Paul shook his head at his own bad behavior.

"Maybe we're more alike than we know. Maybe it's this house; it can make you think differently," reasoned Elia, as if she knew what his thoughts were and that she, somehow, was like him. Did they avoid intimacy on purpose, or were they destined to both be here at this moment. Maybe that's why no one before this seemed to connect?

They both looked at each other and the intensity of the moment, and Paul shook it off.

"Yeah…. so go on, tell me the story. I gotta know everything now," Paul asked, intrigued.

They sat on the porch looking like an old married couple. Even they found it hard to believe that they had only met less than twenty-four hours ago. Elia let out a gentle sigh, and settled in to tell her long story.

"So, Captain Edwin Harrison, he built this place, was this dashing, wealthy, and well-educated man, in his late fifties by the time he took the trip back to Japan to gather up his new young wife. The woman he finally married was too young when they first met ten years earlier, but Captain Edwin finally fell in love with her on one of his trips to Chiba, Japan. She was the eldest daughter of Edwin's Japanese partner. Everything had to be perfect, above board, you know?" Elia seemed to tell the story as if she were there, or had heard it many, many times.

"Chiba? What's a Chiba, Elia?" Paul leaned in to her; he was waiting anxiously to hear the rest of her tale.

"That's the village where Oshima, that was her name, grew up in Japan. It's a village that made the best samurai swords for generations; perfect craftsmanship. In Japan, Oshima's father went into business with Edwin; they used his abandoned sword factories and started making steak knives and selling them to the Western world. Edwin made a fortune on these knives; they were supposedly crazy beautiful and sharp beyond belief. So, while he and his partner were building this business, the Captain purchased a beautiful spot on the Sausalito waterfront from his old friend, William Randolph Hearst. It was right here, that he built his house, this sweet old white Victorian from the ground up."

Elia told the story as if she were there, a living witness to the story as it unfolded.

Elia sipped some of her coffee and continued. "So his partner,

I think his name was pronounced Chinju, the Japanese village leader, actually nudged Edwin towards his daughter, Oshima. The Captain had brought a lot of money to the village and was pretty well known back then. There are lots of articles written about him. His nickname 'Pearl' came from the fact that he imported more pearls from the orient than any other merchant of his era. That's how the house got its name; first they referred to it as Pearls' house, than over time it became the 'House of Pearl.' We found some articles about him here, up in the attic. I'll show you later."

Elia's voice began to trail off and Pearl's voice took over the story. Paul became mesmerized and taken to another world. He felt lost with intrigue as the story continued. Now, the house had become pure white and the morning daylight of the outdoors darkened and became tinted with a deep violet.

Seemingly transported to another time and place, Paul found himself enveloped by an ancient Japanese melody. He sensed the music was Elia's voice and his own imagination took him to another world, far, far away.......

It was Japan in 1878, and the deep violet of dawn was slowly fading from the East. A low melody emanated among the lush, green hills. The melody became a low, deep, resonant sound... the sound of morning ritual bells. Gong, gong, gong greets the morning. The sun continued to rise over the rolling multi-colored hills of this seaside village near Chiba, Japan.

Shinto shrines dotted the landscape and the thatched houses were beautifully designed to fit into the lush, dense forests and fields of rice paddies. Moss covered the rocks and small pathways that led villagers from one house to another as well as into the village center. It was a beautiful and peaceful place. As the morning sun hit a ridge above the village, three young women, two dressed in colorful, silky robes and the eldest oddly dressed in crudely made buckskins from the American West, were gathered in a close group. Their hair was pulled back in simple ponytails, and they worked on their bonfire on this ridge above their home. They laughed joyously, and by their posturing, they were similar in look and movements, maybe sisters. One of the girls, Oshima, the tallest of the three, was painting at an easel. A bonfire had kept them warm while they waited for the sun to come up. Down the hillside, smoke rose from the chimneys of the thatched roofs of this small industrial village.

The bell's resonance shortened and blended into the bells on Captain Edwin's diminutive pony, ringing as his horse stumbled up the trail. Captain Edwin was on horseback, not a familiar activity for this now almost fifty year-old seafaring man, but he was dashing and handsome and his confidence made him very desirable.

A young Japanese man rode up on horseback and encircled the Captain. "Hello Neko-san," Captain Edward said as he greeted the man.

"Hello, Edwin-san. You need to get a real horse next time. I will ride ahead and alert my uncle."

"Thank you, my friend."

The elegant and beautiful Oshima, Chinju's sixteen-year old daughter, was enjoying painting along the ridge that sheltered the village. Her two sisters, Miyumi and Hatomi stood beside her talking as only sisters do, they whispered in each other's ears and giggled. It was a private conversation that only the sisters can share.

"We are so lucky to have a setting like this to paint, Miyumi," observed Oshima.

"I just love being here when the sun comes up," Miyumi added to the conversation.

The youngest sister, Hatomi, who shivered from being cold and was bored, was curled up and close to the fire.

"Can we go back now?" as she swatted at some bugs, Hatomi did not feel the same joy at being outdoors as did her sisters.

"Little sister, you need to recognize the great majesty of Mother Nature," Miyumi chastised her.

"I only recognize the majesty of our divine Emperor, big sister. Mother Nature is not," Hatomi whined.

"Where is your imagination? Look at your sister Oshima. Look at the contentment in her eyes; a driving purpose to complete her task," Miyumi said as she shook her head.

Oshima suddenly stopped painting and hurriedly cleaned her brush and started to pack up her gear as she looked down the road.

"Look! Captain Edwin-san is coming up the path. I must hurry. Could you two pack up my things and bring them down the hill?" Oshima asked as she laid everything neatly down in a pile next to her sisters.

"Yes, big sister. I'll bet he's got something really nice for you this time. He always brings something back for you," Miyumi replied.

"I hope he brings me another one of those paintings from France. They are so sophisticated there. Someday we shall see Paris," she coyly replied, and smiled.

"Bye. Thanks," she added as she set off to meet Edwin.

Oshima ran off down the path, she left Hatomi and Miyumi with the cart. Hatomi sneered as if this were beneath her, but Miyumi shut her down right away with a stern "shush."

Oshima had the gait of a gazelle about her as she ran down the path to her house. She loved leaping across creeks and other obstacles in her path. She made three hundred and sixty degree spins while in the air and giggled when she landed smoothly. She was very adept at running through these hills, and her graceful gait and the leather tassels running down the sides of her buckskin outfit made her look as if she was a bird floating in the air as she ran and leaped. She finally reached the men, her stomach fluttered when she saw the man who had captured her heart, which was beating so fast she felt like she was going to faint.

Breathless, "Edwin-san, I am ready to go to California to see the golden streets, and the beautiful women who wear the western clothing! I will look so sophisticated and live like an American. No?" Oshima said boldly and proudly.

"Golden streets? Yes, don't we wish they were, my darling?" He smiled as he looked at her lovingly. "I am very pleased to see you Oshima. You have grown very tall in my absence; you have turned into a lovely young woman. Here, I chipped off a piece of Montgomery Street for you," he said.

"Catch!" he teased as he lobbed a large golden nugget at her. Oshima caught it and admired it while she gave the captain a big hug. She had a schoolgirl crush on the captain, but he didn't notice, or he pretended to ignore it, but her adoration was palpable, and even the servants saw it.

"Oh thank you Edwin-san!" Oshima bowed and smiled as Chinju came out on his porch, and Edwin turned to greet him.

"Come in my friend. Meji has prepared your favorite tea," Chinju said to his friend.

"Thank you my new partner, I am very proud of what we are about to do today. Is the Minister of Internal Affairs going to make it on time?" Edwin replied in perfect Japanese.

The old friends entered the house, which left Oshima outside with her sisters as Hatomi, the youngest and most spoiled of the sisters, had come up from behind and tried to fluster her sister.

"Oshima's in love, Oshima's in love!" Hatomi said, laughing.

But Oshima was unmoved. She didn't care what anyone said as she held onto the golden nugget in her hand, as if it were a long lost treasure. As far as Oshima was concerned it was a treasure, given to her by the love of her life, Captain Edwin.

It was a time of great change for Japan in 1878, especially for the city of Chiba, near Tokyo Bay, on the eastern side of the main island of Honshu. Industrial countries had come in and set up industrial plants to ship their goods out to the West, and Captain Harrison was one of the well-respected pioneers of this practice. His partner, Chinju Ishiku, owned the largest sword foundry and silversmith manufacturing plant in all of Japan.

The Tokugawa Dynasty had been overthrown ten years earlier because of the uneasy transition from isolated feudal Japan to the new globally-integrated Japan. Life had now opened up to the West and many changes were taking place. Many of those changes would make Chinju's factory the first benefactor. Chinju's factory was a prime example of western knowledge having been brought in to assist in the growth of Japanese industry.

It seemed that Captain Edwin Harrison, the great American adventurer and pearl merchant, had come along at a fortuitous time for the Ishiku family. Chinju Ishiku's ancestral knowledge of sword making was no longer allowed due to the outlawing of the Samurai. Officials ten years earlier had locked the doors to his factory and sealed it... until today. But today was to be a great victory for Chinju and his family.

The factory was again ready to open up and forge steel for the Western world in the form of cutlery and steak knives. An endeavor not quite as prestigious as samurai swords once were, but he would now be among the top industrialists in Japan, and that was all the prestige he needed... and Edwin was the key to that success.

This was a proud day for Chinju Ishiku, but he was not dressed in traditional Japanese clothes. Instead, he wore a Western-style dress coat, and big leather boots, and he looked every bit a member of the newly minted westernized Japanese.

Outside, gathered around the entrance to the factory was a large crowd. The Captain and Chinju stood with a Chiba Official as they watched the government officials break the seal and open the doors to the factory. It was an important day for the city, as many jobs would be brought here.

"Enter my family's heritance Edwin-san. It has been ten years since I walked through these doors," Chinju explained in Japanese to Edwin.

"Thank you Ishiku-san, I am honored and excited by what we have started," Edwin bowed to Chinju who bowed back.

They walked through the entrance and down a wide hall. The two men entered the factory slowly while the others waited outside.

Filtered light dappled across the forging equipment, and dust and cobwebs were everywhere. In a heavily fortified room, a vast collection of Samurai swords covered one of the walls. Each individual sword had been made with meticulous craftsmanship, and this wall seemed to be completely covered with them.

Chinju remarked, "As you can see my friend, these rooms are very ancient, some were constructed over a thousand years ago."

Both men walked further into the factory and came to a chamber that resembled a shrine. Chinju pulled out a set of very old keys and opened a very large thick wooden door. Displayed in this room was a very old collection of Samurai swords.

Edwin looked in awe at the craftsmanship shown before him.

"What are these amazing swords?" Edwin asked, he wanted to touch them.

"These have been collected by my family over the last thousand years. Some are said to have mysterious, magical powers. No western man has ever seen this," answered Chinju.

Captain Edwin swept away the cobwebs on one of the cases that housed the swords. He intently admired one sword in particular; Chinju gave him permission to pick it up. Edwin marveled at the lightness of it. The craftsmanship twinkled before his eyes as if the sword had chosen him, to see its beauty. The sword was hand-forged, ancient steel, and the long shaft of the blade's curved edge was still razor sharp. There was a long dragon etched artfully along the upper sheath on both sides of the sword.

Chinju looked surprised at his choice. Chinju, explained the dragon on it to Edwin, and what it represented.

"This is a good omen, my friend. This dragon is Fuku Riu; it is the Dragon King that rules the serpent people under the sea. It will protect you on your long sea journeys."

"This one's impeccable. It's so beautiful. I have no words that can describe it. It is truly a work of art, my friend," Edwin said.

"Edwin, you have chosen well. Most of these swords are hundreds of years old, but that one is a thousand years old. Made by my ancestor, Amakuni, it was forged for the first Shogun's son, Prince Yamato, the warrior that all Samurai modeled themselves after. Many men would kill to get that sword if they knew it existed."

Edwin pulled the blade out of its sheath but Chinju stopped him immediately.

"Edwin-san, don't pull a Samurai blade from its sheath. If you do, it must taste blood before it is returned. It calls for blood if unsheathed." Seventeen stunning rubies encircled by small diamonds ran up each side of the handle imbedded into the golden cording that aided a hand with its grip.

Edwin listened carefully, and did not expose the sword. Solemnly, they left the building to resume their day's responsibilities, and their business deal. The knives were produced and much money was made. Edwin was called back to sea, and begrudgingly he went. It would be another year before Edwin returned for another visit.

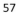

Chapter 7

*T*ime moved on and the business of steak knives grew tremendously, and it was favorable financially for everyone involved. Chinju and Edwin were making more money than they knew what to do with, and Chinju's family wanted for nothing. Chinju was generous and gave support to many of his relatives and towns people, it was a glorious time for the village.

Ten years passed and Captain Edwin "The Pearl" Harrison went back to Japan on his annual trip and found the factory was at full steam and modernized, the locals were wearing western clothes as well as traditional Japanese Kimonos and the small city that had grown up around Chinju's little village was quite impressive. It had become very profitable from the factory.

Times had changed, and Captain Harrison, with large driving goggles on, came up the hillside path riding a motorized bicycle, billows of dark gray smoke spiraled behind him. This was "high technology" at the turn of the century in transportation, and he was one of a few that owned one.

Away from the busy streets and factory Meji tried to find out if Oshima's father, Chinju would finally give his permission for Oshima to marry Edwin.

"Well Chinju what have you decided? Oshima's mind is already in San Francisco. You must let her go." His wife Meji pleaded for his decision.

"Why couldn't we have had a son? What will become of these ancient weapons when they are in the hands of my daughters? Meji, I will miss Oshima deeply, as you will, but she'll come back and visit when Captain Edwin sails this way. They have a wonderful affection for each other, a love that has built up over the years, they are very fortunate, and I give my blessing for her to go." Chinju lamented. He was sad for himself and knew the journey would not be easy for Oshima.

Meji smiled from ear to ear, and a tear dropped from her cheek, she knew that even after ten years, Oshima was still in love with Edwin. Her previously arranged marriage ended tragically a year earlier when she lost her husband to influenza.

The three sisters were painting and writing as they chatted about their lives and desires and the men they would marry.

"Can I change my English name, I don't like Abby? I want to be Elizabeth like the great Queen of England. Oshima, I'm going to miss you so much, who will I speak to in English?" Hatomi asked.

"Who will you speak English with, darling. We will write often and I'll be back with Edwin once in a while." Oshima said.

"I'm sure in time others shall westernize more, my dear Miyumi."

"Maybe, but, I would, too, like to live in America, and leave here, you have found a man you love."

"Oh yes Miyumi, maybe you can come visit me and meet someone too, and yes, I am in love with him." Oshima replied as she noticed Captain Harrison had ridden up from the docks, his merchant schooner was anchored just offshore. She ran back to the village from her perch. Only now she was twenty-six, and in love, and ready for a world-class adventure.

Oshima was dressed in her typical western fashion. Now her Annie Oakley outfit was authentically tailored by a Navajo and shipped back to her, with fringing and beading to die for, all to impress Edwin to show him she was ready for her travels to the wild American West. She ran to the house where her father awaited Edwin.

Chinju was sitting over morning tea and a servant had just told him that Captain Edwin was on his way up from the docks.

Chinju heard a loud motorized sound and moved to the window to watch his old friend who was coming up the hill... Captain Edwin... soon to take his daughter away, maybe forever. Smoke spewed from the exhaust of his motorbike and made quite a racket as he pulled up in front of his old friend's home. Smoke filled the air around him.

Villagers came out of their houses to see the spectacle, a motorbike was a rare sight in this village, and for many, it was the first time they had seen one of these, and to some it was frightening. To some it felt like a dirty dragon had come to take over their souls, and they ran for the hills in their superstitious fear.

Courageous and curious servants and locals moved in slowly and cautiously surrounded the Captain as he turned the machine off and placed the kickstand into a standing position. The smoke swirled around as the Captain removed his gloves and goggles. His friend Chinju parted the crowd as he moved toward his friend, they were happy to see each other.

"Edwin-san you always make a scene wherever you go."

"Well now you too can make a scene, Chinju, this is your new motorbike. I'll show you how it works later. It is my gift to you, old Friend."

They hugged each other and meandered back up to the house. Oshima came running up out of breath.

"If this machine makes this much smoke, imagine what would happen if all of us in this village had one we would be choked to death by the poisoned air."

"You worry too much Chinju."

For months she had worked hard to make her English perfect. Oshima approached Captain Harrison and was thrilled to see him again. "Edwin-san, it has not been so long, and you have forgotten me already?"

"Oshima, is that you? You look so.... you look more beautiful today than I've ever remembered you, and the new cut on your buckskins looks very authentic." Edwin smiled playfully.

"Thank you Edwin-san, I had them made to be like Annie Oakley."

She wondered why he hadn't pulled out a gift for her like he's always done in the past. Captain Edwin and Chinju turned to walk to the house when Captain Edwin suddenly turned back around and shouted out to Oshima.

"Catch!" He threw a small red leather box with gold painted designs on it, at her.

Oshima, surprised and pleased, caught the little box he threw to her. She opened it and it was a beautiful diamond ring, set in platinum. Its brilliance could be seen throughout the courtyard, the servants "oohed" and "aahed" at the sight of it.

Oshima was so excited she cried out in Japanese, "Oh my! It is beautiful, so beautiful!"

"If you decide to keep it you will be coming to San Francisco next spring, your father has agreed to this. We will marry in your custom before I leave and we will be reunited in San Francisco next year. Will you marry me Oshima, I will take you to America and we will live a long happy life. Will you please find it in your heart to marry me?"

Oshima ran up to Captain Edwin and kissed him quickly and she hugged him. Before he could return the affection she was gone, she ran back into the house to show her sisters and her mother.

"Well, I hope we have done the right thing, my friend, San Francisco is very different from here, I hope she will be happy."

"Edwin, you two have loved each other in many ways over the years and now the great Buddha has allowed for your fates to come together in a new and more intimate way. Really, it's quite beautiful my friend."

"I'm glad you think so, it means so much to me. I know she and I will have a wonderful life in San Francisco. San Francisco may be rough, but there is a unique affect that it has on its people. They become, it seems to me, more tolerant, as if the spirit of St. Francis enters anyone who resides there. It is a wonderful place, I will show that to her."

With an arm around his old friend, Chinju set off to the task at hand.

"Come into my house, Edwin-san, we must plan a wedding."

⚓

It was now a time of blessing and happiness and for Oshima's new life with a man she loved. The plans were organized for a lovely wedding and before long, the days had flown by and the wedding day was here. At the Shinto shrine the family and villagers gathered to exchange wedding vows in a traditional Japanese ceremony.

The Japanese bride-to-be, Oshima, was painted pure white from head to toe, she visibly declared her maiden status to the gods. Oshima was wearing a white kimono and an elaborate headpiece covered with many ornaments intended to invite good luck to the happy couple. A white hood was attached to the kimono. Edwin was dressed in a traditional black kimono.

While the bride and groom exchanged their wedding vows: nine cups of sake were finished by the family, as well as bride and groom. After this ritual the newlyweds were then considered united. Extended families and guests also took in the sake ritual to symbolize the bonding of the couple.

The wedding was a dream for Oshima, a dream she had wanted for some time. Soon she would be embarking on her life with Edwin. This would be the happiest day of her life.

"Friends and family, I am pleased to introduce to you, Captain Edwin Harrison and his wife, Oshima Ishiku Harrison, many blessings on this day!" Chinju raised a cup of sake, and it was clear he may have had one too many, but it was allowed, after all, his daughter had just married a fine gentleman from America.

The happy couple was united, and Oshima could not have been happier, as was Edwin, for he truly loved his new bride.

The wedding party made their way back to the house of Chinju, Miyumi and Hatomi followed the wedding party, and then Chinju and Meji. The other guests followed them in ceremonial fashion: there were wealthy guests, factory managers, factory workers, and in the rear were the villagers and common folk who were throwing rice and cheering. The entire village had turned out for the event, and it was a true communal affair! The wedding party wound through the hills from the Shinto Shrine, and they finally arrived at the lavish wedding reception.

The house of Chinju was abuzz with festivities preparing for the wedding party, servants ran around putting the finishing touches on the feast, which was an impressive banquet. The traditional Japanese house was decorated for this traditional Japanese wedding. The entire village had turned out for this very special event, and dozens of workers helped with the reception, musicians, servers and chefs were there too.

Chinju's house was a large one-story wooden structure, it was horseshoe-shaped and gathered at an intricate iron front gate, the house then wrapped around on the inside with a connected walkway, so that when it rained you could walk from one part of the house to another without getting wet. It was simply decorated, but so beautiful in its simplicity. The twenty or so rooms seemed vast, and each room was unique and decorated with different swords and paintings.

Chinju and Meji were beaming with pride as they moved through the crowd now dressed in their traditional Tokugawa Kimonos.

Edwin had brought a western piano player and a piano. This piano player took turns as he played between the traditional Japanese band of musicians, and occasionally tried to play along with them. This led to some very original music, which was eerily similar to Elia's song from the roof.

The wedding reception banquet was served on long low tables, seating for at least three hundred guests. Edwin and Oshima shared the head of the table.

For the wedding reception, the new bride had changed into a red kimono and after the dinner, she changed into a western-style gown. After that, and probably late into the night, she and Edwin would be taken to the honeymoon quarters for their wedding night. Oshima was beside herself with happiness, and everyone there was happy too.

While waiting for her, the wedding party and invited guests engaged in games, and skits during the wedding reception. Guests were expected to offer the couple goshugi -- money -- in a festive envelope either before or after the wedding ceremony. Envelopes with money built up in the corner of the garden, where a swordsman guarded them. Once everyone was seated, servants passed around small trays filled with sake of which each guest was to drink again to celebrate the wedding.

Chinju decided to take Edwin aside and bring him to his armor room. On the wall was mounted a very unique Samurai sword with a magnificent blue sapphire stone mounted on its sheath and a ruby and diamond encrusted handle.

"Edwin-san, I remember you admired this sword the day we

opened the Factory, I have no sons, and Oshima is my oldest daughter. I would like you and Oshima to have this sword so that it may be revered in your family as time passes. It is precious to me, as is my daughter, and it is a great honor for me to give this to you."

Edwin held the sword Chinju had just given him, and as he admired it, Edwin became emotional at the thoughtfulness of the gift.

"I don't know what to say this is an amazing example of another time. I'm honored, so honored. And rest assured my friend, I love your daughter, and I promise I will make her happy, I promise you."

Edwin put the shoulder strap on and the two men left the armor room and re-entered the party.

"Where have you two been? It's time for Edwin-san and his new bride, me, to leave this wonderful party that you have given us father. This could not have been more beautiful." Oshima beamed with pride.

Oshima embraced Chinju and then her mother, Meji. Chinju and Meji stood at the door and watched Edwin and Oshima leave to their quarters, the first time as lovers, now husband and wife.

Their passion was pure and filled with love. Oshima slowly undressed Edwin while Edwin attempted to undress her. She had to undo the complicated Western-style wedding gown; Edwin was like a young man in her presence and their passion ignited in both of them.

Edwin looked at his bride as if he were looking at her for the first time, "Oshima, my sweet and very precious Pearl, we will be so happy. You will want for nothing, and you will be the toast of San Francisco, and America. We will go to New York City."

"Oh! New York?" Oshima squealed excitedly.

"And anywhere else you want to go. Once this last voyage is finished for me, you and I will start a family and live at the house

I built for you. Our future is in that house. We will grow old and see our grandchildren play there. This is just the beginning, my love."

"Oh Edwin-san, I cannot wait, how can I ever pay you back for what you are about to give me?"

"Please, my sweet Pearl, *you* have given *me* everything, and I will love you throughout eternity. You make me so happy, like never before." He smiled at her intently, and she knew he meant every single word.

"I love you too, Edwin, and I will make you happy every day of your life. I love you." She caressed his strong shoulders with her fragile hands, and smiled lovingly up at him.

She breathed heavily and Edwin took her in his arms and kissed her for the first time as her lover, Oshima then lied down in Edwin's bed, and they made love for the first time. He was a thoughtful lover and was very tender with her. After such a long courtship, they were finally united as husband and wife, and they thought that their whole lives were ahead of them……..

Chapter 8

*P*aul listened intently while Elia continued to share this story that was beautiful in parts but sad in others. They sat closer together on the porch. The food and drinks were near an end, so Elia restocked the small table with fresh beverages.

"So, I take it she came to San Francisco, right?" Paul was now thoroughly wrapped up in the tale.

"Yes, she did Paul, but sadly for her things didn't quite work out the way she had hoped." Elia replied topping off Paul's cup. "She had such dreams of passion and a life of marriage in America, but her life instead took a distressingly sad path."

"Sounds interesting," Paul responded. He sipped his drink and looked at Elia, totally interested to hear more. The breeze was mild and the beautifully talented company Paul was keeping was the only thing on his mind as he listened to Elia.

"So, it continued, Oshima was married, but Captain Edwin had to leave Japan before her. He was a man of responsibilities and he had an important expedition to complete. He decided to send Oshima on a ship after he left, then they would meet in San Francisco the following spring."

"Nice honeymoon," Paul let out sarcastically.

"I know, right?" Elia continued, "But he left her in the capable hands of one of his sailing colleagues, First Mate, Prescott

MacGregor. Prescott was much younger than Edwin and he was ruggedly handsome as well."

"Uh oh. I sense trouble coming."

"Exactly!" Elia nodded in agreement with Paul and looked off towards the bay. The lilting of the soft breeze and rhythm of the swells took her back in time and she continued the story of Oshima.

⚓

It was now early spring and Oshima looked around lovingly at her father's house for the last time. She felt a sense of sorrow to leave such memories behind, of growing up with her sisters and her parents but she knew a new life was awaiting her in America with Edwin. It was time to leave and Oshima, with her entire family and her luggage left for the harbor, where the SS Dakota awaited her.

Her father and mother were melancholy, Miyumi cried inconsolably, and Hatomi smiled, knowing that with her older sister gone, she would be closer to a husband and a wedding of her own, and that pleased her.

The SS Dakota was built during shipping's "Golden Age," designed from the drawing board to the docks to be a preeminent luxury liner of that era. Edwin had spared no expense to make sure her voyage was First Class all the way.

Oshima's cabin had a private balcony, and the large stateroom had a separate parlor and bedroom. She would be able to entertain guests in the large salon and even have small dinner parties if she chose. The main parlor had two large comfortable couches, upholstered in a deep rich red and gold jacquard that felt like silk to the touch from her hands. The tables were intricately carved with exotic designs, made of deep rich mahogany. Her room was plush and comfortable. Her family was now standing on the land as she was moving away from it and she lamented for everything she had ever known and loved, she was leaving it all behind.

Oshima settled down in a big soft silk upholstered chair and concentrated on her feelings, trying to embrace the new adventure she was now embarking on. A world she really had no knowledge of, other than postcards, paintings and some information she was told. Oshima knew it was to be a new life, different from her quiet life back home and she would be with Edwin, who she had known for many years.

In an ornate keepsake music box, Oshima unfolded pictures of her family. In one, Oshima and her sisters were formally sitting with her parents. She had pictures of her town, their home, and Japan. She also had a picture of her late first husband, Noburu. How strange that she had another man before Edwin. She did care for him, but not like Edwin. She married Noburu thinking that Edwin would never accept her, and after all, she wasn't getting any younger and the prospects for an aging and unmarried Japanese woman were bleak. At least as a widow she could keep property and live as she wished. She thought of her family, how could she have room in her heart for so many people, especially two men? What a scandal. She knew she loved Edwin before she met Noburu, but he was so sick and died so quickly after they married that it almost seemed like it was someone else. She put the pictures away and felt, the longer she looked at them, the sadder she would get, after all, she had a new life ahead of her. All she had to do was get through the next months and next year at this time, she would be with Edwin.

She had barely left Japan, but she felt the loss already. As she looked out of her stateroom window, the island of the rising sun was a small lump on the horizon and the family that had been there every day of her life was now miles away. A teardrop fell down her cheek. Going through her keepsake box she found her pearl necklace, and her personal diary. These treasures were hidden in finely crafted compartments that slid out on the side of the music box.

Oshima looked around her quarters and noticed the wait-staff had unpacked her suitcases and her clothes hung neatly in the cupboard. Her luggage was stacked neatly against the wall and she felt homesick already. There was nothing familiar about her surroundings. Nothing comforting or nurturing, just new furniture empty of old friends and a dream of her new life as Edwin's wife.

Oshima knew it would be a long journey and she had never been away from her small Japanese island. She had so many questions swirling around in her head. Would she be scared? Would she be lonely? Would there be a storm? How would Edwin be when she arrived? Would he still love her when she stood next to the high society ladies of San Francisco? Would she be a novelty that he soon tired of? Thoughts ran through her head like a freight train, so much so that she felt dizzy, and then she realized that she hadn't eaten a thing for almost the entire day. She was famished.

Interrupting her reflective thoughts was a loud rhythmic knock on her door. She slowly stood up and went to the door. She looked through the sliding peephole, but only saw the back of a man's head. He was dressed in a ship's uniform, and seemed to have a high rank.

"Yes?"

"Missus Harrison?"

Oshima was confused for a split second before remembering that she was, in fact, Mrs. Harrison. How strange this felt to her.

She stood still behind the door, and somewhat afraid, Oshima asked, "You know Edwin... Captain Harrison?"

"Yes, ma'am, he asked me to watch over you."

"Yes, hold on, please." She looked around at the room, everything seemed in its place, so she would receive him now.

"Yes, please come in."

First Mate Prescott MacGregor entered the parlor area, and looked around. He was impressed at her lodgings.

"This worked out well, I must say. I knew you would like it." He said proudly, as if he was the one who made the arrangements.

Oshima now saw the young man, very broad in the shoulders and adorned with colored ribbons and medals of all kinds. He had thick black hair with long thick sideburns, and was tanned from years at sea, and his clear blue eyes made him quite handsome. He didn't have the years of rugged sea life like her husband: he looked so young and fresh-faced. He was taller than her husband, and Oshima was surprised that she was comparing him to Edwin, and she didn't even know this man. She stepped back a little.

MacGregor looked at Oshima and extended his hand, "First Mate Prescott MacGregor, My Lady, and I will be your First Mate. Your husband asked me to look after you on this voyage. I am here to get you anything you need. I.... am at your service."

Oshima looked at his hand and she took his hand shyly as she was not used to this type of attention. *After all, Americans shake hands, don't they?*

"How do you do?" She asked, she felt a sense of comfort from their hands touching.

They had now been formally introduced and she now knew there was someone around she could talk to if need be. Prescott left the room and Oshima freshened up to explore the ship.

⚓

Society ladies and fine gentlemen packed the bars and gambling halls of the ship, all dressed in velvets and silks and fine woolens. In First Class, although she had a fine wardrobe, Oshima felt out of place. She began to spend solitary days on the upper deck of the ship and watch the ocean roll by. She tried to decide what mythical creatures the clouds were forming into, instead of chatting to anyone.

Oshima found some solace on this long journey from the library on the second deck. She read the popular novels of the day, *Little Women*, *Wuthering Heights*, The *Adventures of Tom Sawyer*, and her favorite, *Jane Eyre*. She could be in new worlds and adventures without interacting with the confident and self-assured ladies of the ship. The ladies for their part, had not tried to befriend her, she was like an invisible passenger, although obviously wealthy, being Japanese, she did not fit in, and this was painfully obvious to her.

Even with her books and waiting for her husband, she longed for her family, and felt deep pangs of loneliness. She became more and more depressed as the days passed. It occurred to her one day, that her loneliness was consuming her: she had never been so lonely. Her parents, sisters, or personal servants had always been around, they loved and cared for her. But now there was no one. It began to make her feel inconsolable.

Late one rainy day on deck, Oshima sat on a chaise under a protective awning, wrapped in big woolen blankets and cried herself into a deep sleep. She was exhausted emotionally and physically as the journey was taking its toll on her. She slept many hours open to the harsh elements. When she awakened, she was practically frozen and she shivered with fright and coldness. Her frozen state went straight through to her bones and she was chilled to the core.

The sky above the sea had turned dark and it seemed that no one cared, why she was there, she wondered had she done the right thing? She had sunken deep into despair when she saw a light coming down the aisle, and heard a man's footsteps, she tried to move but was frozen in place by fear and the cold. The light had gotten stronger and after she hid her eyes, she looked up. Her wide eyes looked up to see the only person she really knew on the boat: Prescott MacGregor. He had come to save her.

"Dear God, My Lady, what are you doing out here? You're nearly frozen to death. Come now," Prescott said as he swooped her up in his arms and carried her to her cabin.

His footsteps were swift and sure as he held her, she felt his warmth and she buried her face in his big warm chest.

"Oh Prescott-San, what am I to do?"

"Get you thawed is the first thing."

When he reached the cabin with her in his arms, he called out to a butler who was patrolling the hallways, "Charles, get some hot soup, tea and sandwiches for Mrs. Harrison right away, she's been on deck all night long. Rush now, man."

The butler Charles nodded in agreement and rushed towards the kitchen.

As Prescott reached the cabin, he put Oshima on the couch next to the fireplace in the parlor. He rubbed her arms and legs to get her circulation going and tilted her head up to see if she was all right. Small icicles had formed on her cheeks from her crying. She had been sad, but she would be fine now so she strained a smile back at him.

"Now, you promise not to do anything like that again, Misses Harrison. Please?"

"Oshima, my name is Oshima."

"I know, it's a beautiful name, Oshima." As Prescott said her name for the first time, he said it with a special fondness and Oshima smiled up at him, yes, she was getting better.

There was a knock at the door and Prescott answered, Charles the butler had a rolling tray of soups, teas, warm biscuits and sandwiches, certain to warm her up.

Prescott thanked the butler and they were again left alone. Kneeling down before her, Prescott took off her boots, and rubbed her feet. He massaged her calves, and his tender strokes made everything better.

"Why are you so nice to me? Everyone hates me on this ship."

"No they don't, they just don't understand you, that's all."

"What? That I am some strange foreigner that has married a rich American for his money?"

"No, that's not what they think."

"What do you mean?"

"Well, you don't try to talk to them, you know, they aren't sure if *you* like them."

"But, my English is not so good, and I am, I am not like them. The women here are so beautiful and strong. In Japan, women aren't like that."

"You are strong, look at you, you are very strong. You left home for a new country not knowing if you would ever come back, or see your family again, and you did that by yourself. You got on this boat by yourself. That's pretty strong if you ask me."

Oshima now realized she may have been seeing things from the wrong point of view. "Maybe, but what can I do?"

"I'll teach you."

"Teach me what?"

"Well, let's start with having some fun, a card game, Poker?"

"What is poker?"

"Perfect." Prescott walked over to the parlor's armoire; it contained drawers of cards and all the games you could imagine. Dominoes, cards, mahjong, checkers, chess, you name it, it was there.

"Let me teach you how to shuffle a deck of cards, once you learn that, you'll be the Belle of the Ball, My Lady, the Belle of the Ball..."

Hours later, Prescott had taught Oshima the rules and strategy of poker, and as they played, she laughed and found herself having fun for the first time since she left her family back in Japan.

Oshima was exhausted, Prescott gave her a glass of fine port wine to help her sleep, and after she drank it, she leaned over and kissed him on the forehead. "Thank you Prescott, you have made me so happy tonight."

Prescott leaned in closer to her, and his eyes met hers and he slowly and tenderly kissed her on her lips. Oshima did not draw back; she took her arms and at first held his shoulders to keep him away, and then she gave in to her passion and wrapped them around his neck tightly, as if she never wanted to let him go. He kissed her again, and they were locked in a sensuous kiss that seemed to go on forever. Oshima swooned and was lost in the moment and her passion for this man who had saved her tonight.

Still in their kiss, Prescott stood up with Oshima in his arms, he was so strong and self-assured, that it was no effort at all, and she was small and light. He carried her towards the bedroom and opened the doors with his foot. As he walked into the room, he gently put her on the bed, and looked down at her. She looked up at him and unbuttoned her jacket and threw it to the side of the bed, she had a white silk shirt on and she slowly unbuttoned it as well until he could see her undergarments of lace, she was very beautiful and she wanted him badly. Her desire for him was all consuming, and he burned for her as well. Her loneliness and his passion had been building for weeks and it was about to be let loose. They were young lovers for the first time.

Prescott stood naked before her and she marveled at his chiseled body and good looks, there was no guilt, no fear, no regret for Oshima, only desire, and she took him inside of her like a starving child.

They made love over and over again for hours, and it was well into the next day when they finally went to the parlor for some food and drinks. Prescott had ordered dinner for them and they ate roast beef and Yorkshire pudding, and drank rich red wine.

"Prescott, I love you."

"I love you too, Oshima, now eat, you need your strength."

They ate and drank like they were famished and went back to bed and made love, over and over again. Hours turned into days, and days turned into weeks.

The long voyage at sea was like an intoxicating dream for Oshima, the pleasures she felt with Prescott were so unlike Edwin, but she was helpless against her new-found love.

He would go to his post during the day, and she would play poker, chess, and checkers with the ladies on the ship who were now warming up to her. She was deliriously happy, and the time now flew by.

Oshima treasured her days filled with games and meeting new people and hearing about their lives and especially the nights with Prescott, where she unleashed a sensuality that she could never have imagined with Edwin.

Edwin... Edwin, he had been on the back of her mind always. What would happen when she arrived in San Francisco, would she still love him, what would Prescott do?

Prescott was everything that Edwin wasn't, and yet, she still longed for her husband. She thought again of how it was possible for two men to be in a woman's heart, she had no answer, but only knew that it was possible.

The night was still as the steamship lumbered toward the northern coast of California, tomorrow they would be in San Francisco, and Oshima and Prescott knew this would be their last evening together. As they lay in bed together, Oshima nuzzled up to Prescott's chest, she felt safe and warm there, and it seemed like she never wanted it to end. But it would end, and it would be tomorrow.

"Oshima, my sweet, I know we have never discussed him, but you know it would never work with us, you are another man's wife. I do love you, but my life is the sea, it's what I do, and I can't change that, it's my course in life, my duty."

Oshima knew this story all too well, and it was Edwin as well whose life revolved around his sea adventures. She now knew that Prescott's first true love was the sea, he was so young, and she was going to be with her husband Edwin, surely he would want to stay home and build a life with her. But for now, she had Prescott, and tomorrow she would start her new life.

Prescott seemed to remember something, and slowly climbed out of the warm and fluffy bed. He went to his thick woolen coat and pulled out a long leather case from the side pocket.

"I have something for you my love," he said as he handed it to her.

"Oh, Prescott, you shouldn't have," Oshima blushed.

"Well, it's not what you think."

As he said this, she opened the box to reveal a leather sheath with a small fine dagger in it. She looked at him quizzically, "I don't understand."

"I had it made especially for you, look," he went over to her undergarments and picked up her corset.

"You see, it goes right here," as he said this, the small sheath fit perfectly in between the grommets on the inside of the corset, and one could not even tell it was there. It was beautifully crafted of gold and hand forged steel.

"I want you to always feel safe, and you never know if you're going to need this. He will go away on journeys from time to time, and this will be with you always. You can remember me and with this, I will always be with you too. I will be there to protect you."

"Prescott, I don't know what to say," Oshima said matter-of-factly.

"I know it's not romantic, but Edwin would know if you have jewelry that he had not given you, and I just worry about you being alone. That's why."

"Oh, it is beautiful, and very thoughtful. Thank you Prescott," she reached up for him and embraced him long and hard.

They made love for the last time that night: they shared an intimacy they had not felt before. They knew tomorrow they would have to leave each other, but tonight they enjoyed being together.

⚓

The SS Dakota arrived in San Francisco to all the pomp and circumstance you might expect of a world-class ship. Hundreds of people had lined up to see the ship at the wharf, and families, friends, butlers and wait staff bustled around the ship that was being unloaded. First to exit the ship were the First Class passengers and the society ladies and gentlemen walked down the gangway, it had been a lovely, regal trip for everyone.

The daylight sparkled with the diamonds and gems shining from the ladies as the men laughed and smoked their cigars. A band played lively music and it was very festive indeed. Among the last of the First Class passengers was the exotic and beautiful, Oshima. She said her goodbyes to her fellow shipmates, and they clamored around her to say their farewells.

Oshima gasped slightly as she saw Prescott, waiting for her at the gangway. He was strong and sure standing there, and had seen her immediately.

Prescott MacGregor stood at attention as he escorted Oshima down the gangway, he hid his affection for her.

"My Lady, it has been my pleasure to have been your escort

on your journey, may you remember it fondly, and me, remember me."

"I will remember our time always, thank you Prescott, thank you." She replied looking down from his beautiful eyes. She looked back at him and smiled sadly, she held his hand with both of her small delicate hands. This would be their final goodbye and they would both not let on how they felt about it. No one would ever know, especially Edwin.

Black and gold adorned carriages wait at the docks in the drizzly San Francisco day for their well-heeled patrons. It is cold and wet, and even the porters look drenched and chilled to the bone. She looked up at the city before her, and she saw a figure that seemed familiar, it was Edwin, and under his umbrella he had a large bouquet of red roses waiting for her. He was anxious to bring her to her new home. She ran to him and hugged him hard. She was home, home with Edwin, and now life would be perfect. Oshima's new life was to begin as she had travelled far. She watched Edwin as he sat beside her in their carriage and she smiled, feeling a sense of relief that she had made it. In her mind she said goodbye to Japan, her family, Noburu, and even Prescott. Life was starting anew for her now, and she kissed Edwin's hand tenderly. *Home at last..........*

Chapter 9

*T*he evening was nearing and Paul had not even noticed that he had spent the entire day and previous night, with one woman only. As a player, he would be with various women, day and night, besides Elia's interesting story was fine but he was more interested in staying with her. She made him feel whole, and this was a new feeling for him.

"Dinner needs to be fixed, or do you feel like ordering some pizza? Or do you have anywhere else that you need to be?" Elia asked and looked at him with an inviting smile.

"I have no other plans but you, Elia, besides I like your story, how does Oshima's life in San Francisco turn out? Did they have any children?" Paul asked, he called a pizza take-out near the club he frequented "one large Maui Zowie thanks, with extra cheese." He hung up his phone. "Now that that's solved, let's open some wine and you keep telling me this story, okay?"

Elia brought out some more wine to the porch and they continued to sit in the light evening breeze as the twilight arrived.

"Oshima's life took a horrible turn." Elia stated as she poured the wine and continued to chat about this story.

⚓

Oshima had been enjoying her new life with Edwin. She had begun to improve her English and broaden her areas of interest and knowledge, of the arts in America and worldwide. They both were extremely happy just living their day-to-day lives together, when Edwin had to set out once again on one of his voyages.

On one foggy cold evening, Oshima and Edwin were in their elegant dining room: they talked of their day together.

Oshima asked quietly, "Edwin-san, when we have children they will be strong and smart like you. I will give you a child when you return, I know it."

"And gentle and lovely like you, my Pearl." Edwin replied with a tender smile. Although he was such a fierce man, with a stubborn reputation, when he was with Oshima, his defenses were down and he was a kind and gentle man. He loved that she made him feel this way, only one person had the key to his heart, and they were here together, married and ready to start a family.

"I think I will have a boy first, Edwin the Second, and then two girls, so that he may watch over them. We will have many grandchildren and take them to Japan often. Can we do that, my love?"

"Yes my Pearl, of course. Our son will be a great explorer, and the girls will be the finest ladies of all. They will be like their mother, a rare beauty indeed." Edwin's lust for his wife grew more intense.

He stood up and walked down to her end of the long mahogany table and sat down in a chair next to her.

"Let's try to make a child tonight, my Pearl, may that be the gift I give to you before I leave. Then, when I return, we will have that family. I will never go again, I promise this will be the last trip, we'll have enough money and I can hire someone to captain my ships. From then on I will leave that to the young men. You and I will be together forever, I promise. Yes?"

"Yes, my love." But Oshima was anxious about this trip like no other trip before.

Oshima looked sad at the realization that he would be leaving again. Every time he left, she went into a deep depression, but if she had a baby, he would stay next time.

Yes, this time next year they would have a baby and Edwin would be here forever, never to leave her for his ocean journeys. Next year everything would be perfect..... *next year......*

They made love that night and Edwin slept soundly while Oshima watched him sleep. She knew she wasn't pregnant, she was too anxious, they'd have to try again after he returned. She couldn't get rid of her dread at seeing him leave; she knew it was what he loved to do and that as an adventurer, this was his job, but this would be the last time. He had promised he would be back and she had to hold on to that, but tonight he was here and they were together. Who knew how long it would be before she would be like this again with him. She treasured these last hours together.

She snuggled up under his neck for their last night together.

⚓

The next morning, Edwin's bags were packed and he was ready for another voyage. He walked down the stairs of the front porch, and waved goodbye as Oshima watched.

Once again, she was alone, she had lost Prescott, and now she was losing Edwin. Her family was far away from her and Oshima's new home seemed large and empty to her as she watched Edwin leave. She loved their modern life together and they were making plans for this new life, he promised he would be back as soon as he could and left Oshima in the house as he went about his duties abroad.

Oshima shivered as she waved to Edwin, she turned, closed the door and went to the parlor and sat by the fire and waited for her husband to return.

Weeks had passed and it seemed Oshima's fate would be horrifically ended, and the dreams and plans Edwin and she had made where to be lost forever.

News came to San Francisco that a band of marauding coastal pirates had been terrorizing locals and that the police had been called out many times to arrest the derelicts. They would rob from wealthy and poor people, but they tended to harm no one. But concern was growing as they had become more brazen and violent, Oshima was afraid of being all alone in her big, regal house next to the wide-open waterfront. She had always disliked being there alone, but now she was even more afraid.

Close to the Golden Gate and the Pacific Ocean, the House of Pearl was easy pickings for a fast moving sloop to come in, take what they wanted and just as quickly depart. This band of pirates, headed by the dangerous Louie Lorant, moved in quickly, they had come to rob the house, because Edwin was known to be away. A murderous pirate named Cutfish was with Louie, and his brutal pack of pirates. Cutfish was a short, dark and greasy looking pirate, one could tell he had no scruples nor did he care what anyone thought of him.

After the pirates broke into the house, the home was being ransacked of every fine jewel and collectable. From her bedroom at the back of the house, Oshima heard the chaos and went to the hallway to see what was going on, She opened the door slowly until she could see what was going on. There were strange men in the house and it surely wasn't Edwin. It could only be the criminal pirates on another one of their raids. She had to find a way out. They had no respect for anyone, they were vicious and they enjoyed their work.

The home was being damaged and vandalized as Louie wandered off for a moment inspecting an old Samurai sword that was mounted over the fireplace. He took it down and was startled by how cold it felt.

As the pirates moved through the house, Cutfish screamed at the top of his lungs, "Here, here, there's someone in the back bedroom! Get her, grab her, she's gone out the back door!"

The men ran out through the back door to the back terrace and tackled a terrified Oshima as she was trying to make her escape up a trellis in the back and up the cliff behind the house and then onto the road above the house.

"Get away, take what you want, just let me go!" she screamed at her captors as she tried to get away from their grasps. Unfortunately for Oshima there were no neighbors near enough to hear her screams, muffled by the cliff and the waves beating against the shore.

They dragged her into the main parlor, where Louie was standing by the raging fire; he devilishly looked at her and licked his lips. He was holding her husband's treasured sword that her father had given to him when they married. The pirate spoiled the sanctity of the blade with his touch.

"Cold, very cold," Louie said in French and turned to show the sword to Oshima when he saw one of his men had touched her on her neck and breasts. Louie pulled out the sword and shoved it through the side of this foolish pirate's neck and pushed it clean through while he whispered into the dying pirate's ear. Blood spewed from this man's neck, down Oshima's front, as the man stood in shock.

"I said, nobody goes near her, you 'vache couvir.' What are

you doing? Huh. How does this feel? Now that you go to meet your maker, you'll understand no, when he says no, to heaven for you, my smelly whoremonger friend." He threw the dead pirate aside, pulled out the sword, and wiped it off on the dead man's clothes then replaced it into its sheath. The sword was warmer now. Louie then straddled Oshima's lap as she cried and pleaded for her life.

He whipped out the strand of pearls that he had taken from her jewel box and he wrapped them around her neck and strangled her until she fainted, then he pulled her head toward his stomach.

"Come here Cutfish, what is it that you really want?" Louie posed to Cutfish as if he were giving a dog a bone.

Cutfish was extremely stupid from multiple head injuries and years of opium and alcohol consumption, as seen by the many scars on his head and the moronic look on his face. He looked dimly at Louie, "The girl, my captain, the girl, she is what I want, please...."

"The girl, *my captain*, that's what I like about you Cutty, you show me the respect I'm due. That's why I am going to let you be the last pirate to bugger this little fire-stick. Then, when we're done with her, we'll help you get her up into the attic so you can have your way with her, then hide her body up in the attic. If you take too long, we'll leave you behind, and we'll take your share of the booty. Now is that not a show of love, eh, Cutty, my boy?"

"Oh thank you, my captain!"

"No one can ever, ever find her, do you have that?" Louie stated emphatically.

"Oh yes, my captain, yes!!!!" Cutfish said lecherously.

Now tied up in the attic and with her eyes red and swollen from her tears, Oshima had been trying to cut her bindings with the dagger that Prescott had given her while on the S.S. Dakota. Prescott had fashioned a small sheath for it that fit tightly in the bodice of her corset, you couldn't even tell it was there, Oshima tried to take it out many times this evening but it was always just inches out of her reach. Her fingers clawed at her back as she tried to get at it.

"Help me, Prescott, please help me," Oshima said quietly.

Cutfish came up into the attic. The other pirates had tied her up tightly and put her up into a crate for him since they already had molested her. They immediately left down the ladder.

"My turn, my turn, I'm going to hide you," Cutfish said lecherously, "don't try anything funny, I don't want to have to kill you. Oh! I guess that threat doesn't work so good now, does it? It's off to the crate for you. What's so special about all this hard work I'm doin', I could use a little help, but nooo, Cutty go fetch this, Cutty go fetch that."

Cutfish slid her crate over to a dark secluded corner of the attic and found an old abandoned pile of straw which he packed around her. He became more agitated as she squirmed.

Cutfish exclaimed to Oshima, "You're very lovely, my pretty." As he said this, he ripped her bodice open and revealed her soft milky white skin; he licked one of her breasts and Oshima cringed at his violation of her. Cutfish now reached his hand up her skirt violently and grabbed at her upper inner thigh, Oshima screamed, but no one could hear her, not up here. He pulled and ripped off her undergarments, he smiled lecherously the whole time.

Cutfish then pulled his pants down and entered her, it was not easy for him because of his diminutive size and she was fighting him with all of her strength. He was now inside her and he raped her, he laughed and drooled, he was disgusting as his grunts become louder and louder. As he climaxed, he belted out a loud moan and laughed at his conquest. Oshima turned her head in disgust.

Cutfish smiled at her like a rabid dog that had just eaten his meal, "There we go now, that wasn't so bad. Was it?"

Oshima kept searching for the dagger that was so close but hard to get a grasp of, she was trying to grasp it but couldn't get a good grip! She thought about how angry Edwin was going to be and then stretched out as far as she could; she had the handle now in her fingers.

Moving her had dislodged the knife out of its sheath on the back of her corset, and just enough for her to get a hand on it and cut her wrist bindings. So she started cutting.

Having a sudden flash of insight, that he was being duped by his shipmates and that they were probably on their way out of the house and with his portion of the treasure, Cutfish decided to kill Oshima quickly and get back to the ship before they left him behind and took all the loot.

He reached over Oshima to pull the lid down on her. He was agitated and distracted.

Cutfish squealed like a pig, "Oh those sneaky bastards they're going to leave me here and take my share. What am I doing? I've got to go, now."

Cutfish sneered at Oshima "Sorry I can't violate you once more before I kill you. I guess that's just too bad for you." He looked at her hatefully, as if he couldn't stop his own violent nature.

As Cutfish pulled his knife out of his own sheath, Oshima put all of her strength into it and cut the ropes that bound her hands together. In the same instant he struck her, his knife slit her throat. Oshima began to look pale as the blood rushed out of her body, as she realized that her throat had been slit, hers eyes opened widely and with the dagger in her left hand, she shoved it into Cutfish's neck, right through his carotid artery. Blood pumped from the pirate's neck and it was a split-second before he realized he had been cut.

Cutfish gurgled, "Ouch! Now why did you go and do that." Cutfish pulled out her dagger and an even bigger stream of blood streamed out. He was now gushing blood from his neck and his mouth as he tried to stop the bleeding. He went into shock.

Oshima was dying and though she fought back, she wasn't afraid. They had taken her dignity and she knew she was going to take him down with her. If she was to die, she found consolation in the fact that she had taken the vile Cutfish with her.

She pushed hard against the heavy lid trying to gain strength, but she was weak from the injury she had. Her arms couldn't hold the lid open of the old rum crate that she had been placed in, and as the life began to drain from her, she settled down in the straw, becoming too weak to stop the lid slowly closing down on her. Darkness enveloped her.

As Oshima wandered off into a dream-like state, one that was now coming with her death, she vowed that she would keep this house safe from the evildoers who had perpetrated this upon her, her husband, and the House of Pearl. She would never rest until the house was free of these beings, no matter how long it took.

Outside of the trunk where Oshima was dying, Cutfish was holding his hand on his own throat, but it increasingly bled out and he began to get dizzy and weak losing his balance. He fell back away from Oshima and he threw the knife into her trunk just before her lid closed.

He tripped and fell back onto what was to become his secret tomb. Left over lumber and old unused doors fell on top of him. He shuddered as the weight of this wood and the doors crushed him and trapped him in the attic along with Oshima.

Poor Oshima had met a horrifying fate and her murderer had been killed by her hand too. The house moved and creaked in anger, as if possessed, to try and alter this wrong. A paranormal occurrence was beginning to take shape and Oshima and her murderer would now be trapped as spirits in the home's walls.

Oshima saw the world around her moving as she realized she was not in the world of the living anymore, but cursed into a paranormal existence and now, how could she ever see Edwin again? She was in-between worlds, dead and yet still here; her sadness took over her like a wash of warm water.

She was angry and saddened, and as she lay dying in the darkness of her soon-to-be tomb, she thought of Edwin and the life that they would never have. She cursed the pirates for the children she had not yet conceived and prayed for Edwin to find her. As she turned into the netherworld, her prayers became a chant, and now she was nothing but a mere ghost an ethereal spirit, and the house that she once loved and shared with her beloved Edwin, fell around her and embraced her sadness and anger as if they were one in the same.

The house would be now and possibly forever possessed by Oshima's sadness, anger, and spirit.

Chapter 10

$\mathcal{T}$he conversation with Elia was fascinating Paul as he took another long sip of his wine and finished the glass's volume, he then took the bottle and filled both the glasses full. He seemed to need a drink after this story.

"I can't believe such a violent end came to Oshima, are you telling me she is still trapped *somewhere* in this house, right now?"

"Whoa, hold on Sherlock... I have more to tell you."

Elia sipped her topped-off glass of wine and chatted about the home and how strange this place was and that she never believed in paranormal activity, until after what happened to her and her grandmother.

"The story continues Paul, after Oshima's death, the captain lamented his lost passion, and was still obsessed with her. They never found her body and he kept thinking that she had been kidnapped and was still alive, but probably deep down inside he knew she was dead, and gone forever." Elia thought long and hard about the next part.

"He wanted to find her, to reunite with her and he decided to go to San Francisco to find out more about her and what had happened. Paul, he did something I am too afraid at this point to even consider."

"What did he do? What is it Elia"

"He had a séance?"

"Why would he do that?"

"I don't know Paul, I guess to get answers... get in touch with ghosts that might be able to help... he was desperate and angry. I know this house can give up answers if you try hard enough... and I do think this house still has more to tell me. Maybe... we should do one?"

"I think you're great Elia, and I support your ideas, but you're the one who seems to know what feels right. I'll get behind any decision you make. You realize you may not find out anything or you may find out something that is more horrible than you can imagine. I have to say El, I don't do well with this sort of thing. You don't want to find something that you can't get rid of." Paul obviously didn't like the idea of a séance, and he didn't hesitate to tell her.

"Maybe so, and that's exactly what I'm afraid of, and that's why with you now I might have the courage to try it again. OK?"

"Again?"

"Yeah, but I'll get to that later."

"Tell me what happened to the captain. He was still hoping to find Oshima, you say he comes back to find her and then..."

Elia began to tell Paul about the Captain's return from his final voyage and how happy he would be to arrive home and begin his new life with his wife, Oshima.

Elia started telling her tale again, "As you figured Paul, things were not as he had expected them to be. He came home to find a ransacked house and blood everywhere, but no Oshima. The neighbors couldn't help because they were few and far between, with the House of Pearl being located so far from the town center.

The police were also of little help. It's not that they didn't want to help, it's that they had nothing to go on, just the pirate's nicknames and some traces of their presence. But she was gone and there was no sign of her."

Paul grabbed his glass of wine, and settled in for the next chapter of this grim story.

"For months Edwin stayed in their bed, he covered himself in her clothes that still smelled of Jasmine, of Oshima. He barely ate, and drank himself into oblivion almost every night."

Paul shook his head in sadness for Edwin.

Elia said dejectedly, "He was tortured by what had happened to her, and failing his friend Chinju to protect his daughter."

⚓

It was now the fall of 1896, and after months of incoherency from an excess of drinking constantly, Edwin managed to clean himself up and vowed to find Oshima, or at least avenge her, or die trying.

Late one evening, and after many inquisitions, the Captain had gathered some friends around a large round table set in the middle of the main parlor room of the house to begin a séance. He was still a very popular and influential man, and his friends were some of the brightest and most famous people of their day. This was a group of intellects, writers, and of course, a psychic.

The guests began to take their seats and took refreshments prepared for the evening's event. Scotch and ale were poured, cigars were lit, and the vast fireplace crackled with a warm fire.

The Captain switched off the lights: the room was now lit only by the fireplace and the numerous candles that were burning and scattered about. Because of the extensive cigar smoke and crackling fire the room's shadows gave an amazing three-dimensional look to it. The mood in the room became serious as the paranormal ambience of the parlor became very palatable, everyone was eager for answers as to what had happened to Oshima.

Edwin began to speak rather matter-of-factly, "My dear friends, I want to thank you all for coming. I'm hoping we can shed some light on the location of my dear missing wife, Oshima. Our psychic tonight is Flora London. Flora, this is a dear old friend of mine, Ina Coolbrith, she's with the Oakland Library and founded the "Overland Monthly". She brought a couple of writers with her, and old friends of mine, Bret Harte and Mark Twain. I hope you don't mind." He then became more emotional, and it was clear to all that he had lost something very dear to him.

"Flora, I am most pleased to make your acquaintance." Mark replied shaking hands, respectfully. He was a woolly and engaging man, and his southern accent and demeanor brought calm to the room.

"I'm honored by your presence, Mister Twain. I've also brought my son with me, say hello to these fine gentlemen John. He wants to be writer like you Mr. Twain."

This young man, John London, seemed to ignore his mother's request and he slowly stood up to greet these gentlemen. Oddly enough, he too would grow up to be a famous writer.

"Hello, fine gentlemen." John finally said.

"I've seen you before boy, you're that reckless sailor, always beating and humiliating the bigger boats. You bought French Frank's sloop the 'Razzle Dazzle.'"

"Yes, sorry Captain?"

"Don't be sorry boy! For living a feverish life, relish in your exploits, keep a diary, write it down, so in your old age you can read it and relive your youth. Son, you're too vigorous to be a John, from now on I'll refer to you, when I see you, as Jack, yes, Jack it shall be."

John London said kindly, "I like that, thank you sir. Well I just seem to have a hardy understanding of the wind and what it can do if properly harnessed. Nature has many tricks where she convinces man of his frailty – the ceaseless flow of the tides, the fury of the storm, the shock of the earthquake, the long roll of heavens artillery - but the most tremendous, the most stupefying of all, is the passive phase of White Silence. Strange thoughts arise unsummoned, and the mystery of all things strive for utterance... then, if ever, man walks alone, with God."

"That's fine prose coming out of such a young mind." The gentleman Bret replied.

"Oh, it's just a little something I've been working on." John said humbly, and deferred to the other men in the room as he sat back down. They could tell however, that he was a brilliant young man.

"Young John, oh, I mean Jack London, is a voracious reader he comes to my library as often as work lets him. His favorite book is "The African Adventures of Paul du Chaillu."

"It's nice to see a young mind excited by the written word. Remember son that the source for all humor is sorrow." Mark added.

Changing the subject back to the matter at hand, Edwin turned to the lady, "Flora, your purported skills and how you have helped so many people is why you are here, and of course you come very well recommended, if anyone can help me find my precious Pearl Oshima, it will be you. I'm trying to determine what happened to my wife when my house was ransacked by pirates a few years ago. I'm hoping you can help. "

"I will do my best," Flora responded sincerely.

"Well Ina, this should turn out to be a pretty good story. I'm just glad not to be outside on that porch any longer. I swear the coldest winter I've ever known is this summer here in San Francisco." Mark motioned towards a bottle of old Irish Whisky, "You don't mind, do you Edwin?"

Edwin shook his head, "Of course not my friend, just not too much right now."

"We should begin. I have wanted to find Oshima and I need answers. Answers are all that is left for me and the guilt that I have for leaving her alone, knowing she was worried about her new life in this country." Edwin felt forlorn, but he was resolute in that he would find answers and it would be today.

The room went silent and the shadow dancers kept dancing. Everyone seemed to feel empathy for the Captain. For his loyalty to his job and the unfortunate choice he made to leave Oshima that one last time.

The Captain was hoping to source some answers and find peace with what happened and possibly find out where Oshima was now.

The room had a heavy sense of anticipation, as the guests awaited the séance to begin.

"It's now time to begin, please everyone settle, I can feel a presence very near to me. Please advise who you are?"

Now living as a spirit and moving about the house as wisps of vapor, and light winds, Oshima watched below and saw the Captain. She had yet to control this new existence and what she could do with it. Then she saw Edwin and she remembered the affection she had felt with him and being near him. She was now angry. Angry that a bloodthirsty menacing pirate had taken her life. He had ruined the chance she had to live with her husband or to ever touch Edwin again. That ape took her life!

He took her happiness!

He would pay!!!

Seething with anger now, she flew across the room and the candles flickered violently, with some blown out. The guests looked around and searched the ceiling and the room, but no one was searching as hard as Edwin.

"Oshima, Oshima? Is that you? Please talk to me." Edwin said in his tormented state, he scoured the dancing shadows of the room.

"Please if you are Oshima, use my presence as a medium and talk to Edwin; he has tried so hard to find you."

Oshima swept past Edwin, she left his face feeling a shock of cold wind and he heard her voice.

"Edwin-san, sweet Captain Edwin, it's me Oshima... I have been stuck here in the netherworld. Come find me my love, come find me and let me be at peace, I can't stay this way forever... please my love...." her voice floated through the air like whispers from a butterfly in his ear.

"Oh! Oshima, every day I am burdened and sorrowful that you are not here alive, I'm sorry, maybe I should have done something different, as I know how afraid you were."

"If I could have tears I would cry Edwin, as the time we spent together was the most special of my life. Your affection is something I have not forgotten and it drives me crazy trapped here knowing I'll never have you again! That bastard pirate took that away from me... I never wanted that."

"I know Oshima, you were afraid and a pirate you say, tell me his name and I'll kill the scoundrel!"

"He's dead Edwin, the pirate who killed me is dead... Cutfish did the deed and died by my hands, but Louie instigated the order. Seeing you here, I want to touch you and I can't stay near you as it pains me... Edwin-san, I was young and never got to see you again and now I miss you."

"I miss you too Oshima that's why I came and arranged this with the assistance of these fine people. I've always remembered our affection all those years ago and you meant more to me than I told you, but I left you alone... I'm sorry, my love, so, so sorry......" tears streamed down Edwin's face, surprising all in the room at the sight of this rough and rugged sailor as he wept.

"You don't need to be sorry Edwin, we had no choice then...

live your life fully, and my feelings are still real for you, in fact too real, that Edwin, I must leave. Seeing you has made me happy but then again sad, as I cannot touch you, and I long for your touch."

The séance woman's hand moved onto Edwin's hand and affectionately held his palm.

The Captain felt her touch and he remembered it fondly, it made him warm inside at the feel of her. As he smiled and leaned over to talk to Oshima, a gust of wind blew up towards the ceiling. The guests saw a milky transparent supernatural figure vanish into the ceiling and they looked around at each other very slowly as the shadows danced behind them. Mark got up and turned on the lights.

"That was fascinating, how are you feeling Captain?" Mark asked.

"I feel more at peace to have heard her words, but I feel deep sadness that she is lost in this other world."

Flora was revived from her trance "Captain, she has gone and you have to move forward knowing she loves you as you do her."

Edwin looked at her sadly, but was happy for the small moment he had with his love, Oshima.

Their affection during their marriage was intense and closure was here now for Edwin, but he would never forget what could have been. He was sad, but at least he had these last moments with her, even if it was her spirit.

The spirit that was now Oshima could not cry, and she made the house shutter with her anger when he had left.

Edwin told his friends he would come back one day to try to talk to her again, even though they advised he shouldn't. But for Edwin, knowing she was there and he wasn't, was a heavy burden for him to bear. She was there but she was of another world and not real to touch, she was a ghost.

His closure was made and her feelings for him and his towards her were shared, but the thought that she was there and not real to touch anymore, bothered him more than he showed anyone.

While the Captain composed himself, the guests had tidied up and said their goodbyes. As they left the house, Edwin watched them from the porch. He searched for any signs of Oshima, but she was now hiding in the house. Mark Twain had made Edwin promise him to leave the house once the séance was done, and now, Edwin left to regain his life. She saw him walk away from the house. But this house and his wife, Oshima, would forever stay in his heart.

But still, something gnawed away at him: he needed to know who did it, if there was one more thing that had to be done it was revenge. Edwin knew well enough that pirates are like dogs; underneath they are really cowards and must travel in packs to intimidate. He knew where to look for scoundrel dogs, and he would find them.

Somewhere, someone was alive who knew the truth, and if it was the last thing he ever did, Edwin would find him and avenge his beloved Pearl.......

Chapter 11

Outside the air had settled into an evening chill. The view was glistening with small lights across the water and Paul and Elia moved inside slightly intoxicated by the wine.

"You know I should probably get back to the boat tomorrow, I've spent nearly my entire weekend off with you, but you just make me feel like I've never felt before, Elia." Paul said, almost surprised at his candidness.

As Paul moved closer to Elia, he placed his hand around her waist and kissed her. The entire day he had been hoping to accomplish more than a kiss with her, but was too entranced by her company and the story of her ancestors and this strange house. He wasn't one to believe in supernatural forces but he had started to believe that they did exist after her stories.

Elia reciprocated Paul's feelings: she loved his intense passion and as they kissed, they stopped each moment to breathe deeply as they moved around the house entranced in their passion. Their clothes trailed around on the floor. They left a path of where they had been, as they wildly kissed and touched each other's bodies with desire.

The breeze sounded softly through the small openings in the windows that needed repairing and the house began to vibrate with its supernatural elements. It could sense their happiness and desire and it wasn't pleased. Each time their bodies entwined and pushed up against the walls, electrical sparks surrounded them in blazing yellow. They looked at each other and kept on going with their passion until Paul pushed Elia up against a large framed mirror in the hallway.

Elia and Paul had felt their desire once again, they breathed heavily and stared into each other's eyes. She placed her arms up in the air as he kissed her neck passionately.

"This is amazing!" Paul whispered in her ear.

Elia's hands ran across the mirror frame as she stretched out pleased from his soft kisses and she felt a key. She grabbed and pulled it down to look at what it was. It startled her. They slowed down and looked at the key in her hand.

"It's a key Paul, I've never been in this room. Old Stanley or my Grandmother never opened this one up."

"It's a very old style key, let's try it."

Elia slowly turned the key and the door unlocked with a loud click and then creaked opened. It had not been opened in years. The sound of air falling into a vacuum swooshed as the door opened and they peered in. They walked in slowly and peered around and inspected the chairs and beds. It was like it had been vacuum sealed all these years.

"Oh my god, I'll bet this hasn't changed much in more than fifty years. The house was a brothel back in the thirties. Back then, I was told, the local girls would be paraded around for politicians and gangsters like Chicago's Baby Face Nelson" Elia said as she circled Paul.

"Those must have been eccentric days." Paul said as he looked around.

"As it turned out, for a few years, my grandmother and her aunt ran this house, as a brothel. She told me that the experience of selling herself at fifteen, had a huge..."

"WHAT? Did you just say, fifteen? Holy, crap," Paul interrupted Elia in shock.

"...yes! I know scary choices, it was back in the nineteen thirties, it was a brothel! Everyone in my family has led a crazy life, some more than others." Elia looked around.

"Crazy maybe, colorful for sure, no wonder this house has weird vibes."

Paul lay back on the bed nearest Elia as she began telling him of a bygone era of her family's past.

The room was surprisingly clean and dust-free. The ceiling was painted a dark violet and with the dim lighting seemed to be a void, opening to another dimension. The furniture spoke from its own decadent era with plush materials that wrapped around geometric shapes. Extravagant wallpapers covered the walls and thick dark drapes covered up the windows.

"As the story goes Paul, a murder took place in here, of Pearl's parents, my great grandparents. It didn't look like this then, this came along with Aunt Sally."

"How am I not surprised by this... really! I don't think there is anything that could surprise me now, unless I come face to face with one of these supernatural energies." Paul shook his head, and settled in for the next part of Elia's story.

They laid together on the bed and Elia continued the story and told him about this place back in the nineteen thirties.

It was the early 1930s, the house was occupied by Prima Pearl and her mother and father, Christian and Lila Pearl. Lila and Christian had inherited the house from a relative of Edwin's, that was somewhere in their lineage, the name Pearl had stuck as their surname.

One dark night, when everything seemed quiet on the outside, the opposite was occurring here in the home. On this night, another tragedy was to unfold at the house on Bridgeway.

Not seen by the human eye, but felt, was this translucent spirit travelling along the house's ceilings. The ghost was semi-transparent with a milky, fuzzy texture and it freely scatted across the home's ceilings looking for a victim to inflict trouble.

It swirled around the main rooms searching for someone. It floated slowly then darted quickly across the rooms. In some instances it repeated its journey still searching.

It was then when the little girl, Prima Pearl came back to the house. She walked through the downstairs entrance, hung her school bag on the stairs railing and made her way upstairs. With each step she took she had no idea that the ghost was above her following her steps. It floated way above her head and followed her in every room she entered.

"Mommy, I'm home!" the little Prima yelled.

Its transparent milky appearance was not appealing to view and would frighten anyone terribly if you made eye contact with it, she knew nothing and Prima Pearl strolled under it.

The young girl they called Prima was a lovely and striking child, pale with black hair, that flowed and bounced as she walked. She had always been a gifted child, smarter than most, and finely attuned to everything around her. She would often walk quietly around the old house on Bridgeway and listen to the sounds of those of whom only she could hear.

Ever since she could walk, she would sneak up on rooms and look down through the keyholes, sometime she saw things, and sometimes they saw her. Oddly enough, she was never scared and lived with the spirits of the house rather casually: maybe it was that she was a child, simple and with no baggage or hostility, or foibles that the spirits could take advantage of. Whatever it was, today she felt differently, and was unsure as she approached her parent's bedroom door.

Little Prima had heard some noises coming from her parent's room; she peered through the keyhole to find her parents under the sheets as they made love. A ghost slid in through the door and hovered over them. This supernatural force was at a high energy level invisible to most but pushing its forces into this room.

High above on the ceiling, the ghost conjured up a pearlescent sphere from the ceiling plaster. It moved frantically above her father's head, and with exact precision dropped the pearl hitting the father square in the back of the head. Its pearlescence covered the man's body head to toe.

Unknowingly the father continued to kiss his wife as the pearlescence spread over his body and instantly absorbed into his blood stream and he became crazed. His head twisted around, and his laughter was freakishly weird. His body seemed to distort and move oddly energized by a possessed force.

His body moved in ways no human form does and he began to suffocate his wife. Her screams for help vibrated under the sheets as her daughter watched, in utmost terror! She remained frozen, unable to move.

"Christian, what are you doing... no, no, wha-" Lila was cut-off before she could speak. He was strangling her now.

On the other side of the door, little Prima gasped, her left eye pushed up against the keyhole to see better. Her two small hands scratched at the thick wooden door, but went unheard.

His body was too strong and forceful on top of her. She could not move away. She struggled. She struggled more and her eyes glazed over in terror as he continued to suffocate her with the sheets that they were just intimate in. He had no idea he was killing her: he was completely possessed by this sinister apparition that hovered above the bed. Prima began to see the puppet-like ethereal strings that reached up to the ceiling and managed by what appeared to be a sentient fuzzy white cloud.

The white cloud watched from above and vibrated a strong energy of ghastly pleasure into the room.

Poor little Prima watched in horror and disbelief, she was so terrified that her own screams came out as silent breaths.

As she watched through the keyhole, Prima could see her mother's eyes gaping wide with terror as she tried to get air, but her father was strangling her hard with a wild-eyed pleasure that was evil and otherworldly.

Her mother saw her small eye in the keyhole and looked at her as if to tell her to *RUN, RUN...* but Prima watched in terror as the life went out of her mother's eyes and the once bright white eyes were now flushed with black blood that rushed in as she died before Prima's very eyes.

Prima knelt at the door in silent terror.

Her father had killed her mother and then, pulled by the ceiling puppet master, he stepped away from the bed, highly agile but possessed. The ethereal strings that bound him began to break their hold on him. He looked around and started to panic. His human stance was transformed in his gestures; he no longer looked crazed or possessed. He looked at the sheets in disbelief. His eyes swelled with tears of fear as he neared his wife's body, buried under the sheets, he had just murdered her.

He was not himself, he looked about the room to see what had happened, and then realized he had caused this destruction.

He neared her slowly, his hand stretched out shaking. He pulled the sheet back, his eyes cried out with heartbreak to see his wife dead by his own hands. He looked at her. He called her name. He called it again as he shook her, but she was limp and dead in his arms. He cried out loud and felt maddened in his mind. Questions ran through his mind.

How could I have killed her?

Why?

I loved her?

I was making love to her?

What have I done?

How can I live with this?

The answer was, that he just couldn't live with it: he just knew he couldn't. He moved slowly over to the desk in his room and opened the drawer. There was a gun, his gun. He reached in for it and held it to his head. He moved the gun away. Then he looked at his wife and then he looked at the gun.

He was now crying and couldn't bear what he had done.

He held the gun to the temple of his head and as he did, he caught sight of his daughter hidden in the keyhole and he stared in her eyes, apologizing for his madness and he shot himself dead with one shot.

Prima screamed and banged on the door.

Christian's body lay on the ground, blood oozed from his temple, it was a terrible sight to behold, his wife lay dead on the bed, her dead eyes black from her hemorrhaging.

Above the gun-smoked residue the cloudlike apparition seemed to have slipped away. The ghost in the room seemed to be pulled up through the ceiling to another level of the house by an even angrier supernatural apparition.

The house was not pleased with this disastrous tragedy.

After pounding on the door, it finally released its grip on the lock, and the door opened on its own and Prima Pearl slowly entered the room.

Her legs buckled and the little girl knelt on the floor and sobbed inconsolably.

Little Prima was now terrified at seeing ghosts, they weren't her friends and they killed her mother and father. She was shocked to see her father possessed and that he killed himself in madness. She was even more fearful to go closer to see her mother.

Each step she took she kept looking above for that ghost.

She moved closer to her mother and saw her smothered by the twisted load of sheets on her body.

She looked around and saw her parents were now dead and lifeless. She looked above in terror. She was too shocked for even one tear to show. She was weak and in shock from the mad turn of events she had just witnessed, and she collapsed again to the floor.

Chapter 12

"How can you stay here Elia, knowing such craziness?" Paul queried as he looked up at the ceiling as they walked back to the kitchen.

"I don't know why, I just want to find out more about who I am, no matter how crazy it seems. I always thought it was better to live here with my ghosts than to live alone, if that makes any sense at all?"

Paul put his arm around Elia and felt empathy for her situation.

"Wait till you hear the other awful stuff that happened to Prima. That wasn't even the worst of it."

Paul looked aghast again, he knew her story would be even sadder, *"Really?"*

⚓

A few weeks after the tragic death of her mother and father, the house had begun to calm down. The police tape was down, and all the lawyers and police were finished with their jobs, now life would continue. Prima was back in the house after her neighbor, Josephine Standish, took her in while her next of kin was notified. Josephine was a kind woman. She came from old San Francisco publishing money, and was a grand old lady. She too had a young girl, Rosie, who became friends with Prima while she stayed at their mansion in Sausalito.

The day had come for Prima to return to the House of Pearl. So Josephine walked her there with Rosie. "Look Prima it's all painted white and it's as fresh as a new day, no reason to be scared."

"Now you be good little Prima," Josephine said sweetly to the young girl, "Your Auntie Sally is here and she will be taking care of you from now on. It's all settled, honey." Josephine kissed her on the forehead and rang the doorbell at the front door.

The door opened to reveal a hard-looking woman in her 40's, dressed in a bright red gown, highly unusual for this time of day. She had gobs of makeup on and her lips were stained a bright red. Josephine looked up and down at her disapprovingly.

"How do you do, I am Josephine Standish, and here she is, little Prima."

"How do *you* do, dahling Mrs. Standish, I'm Sally Emeral, Pearl's aunt," She extended her hand to shake Josephine's hand and Josephine begrudgingly complied. There was a touch of tackiness in Sally that made Josephine cringe, but this was Prima's family and she couldn't stand in the way.

"Please call if you ever need anything, we are at the house just over the hill," Josephine said as she pointed to a grand mansion on the other side of Sausalito, a house so big you could see it from miles away.

As Prima cautiously approached Sally, little Rosie stepped up to hug her new-found friend goodbye.

"Bye Prima, I'll see you at school?" little Rosie said sweetly, she went up to Prima and hugged her. At ten years old, neither of them could comprehend what really was going on, and that both of their lives would now take very different turns.

"Bye Rosie." Prima said as she was taken into the house, now to be run by her Aunt Sally.

Prima waved goodbye through the window as she watched her new friends walk away, she would now live with the ghosts and Aunt Sally, scared of the new life before her.

Many years had passed since Christian and Lila's deaths, and under Sally's management the house had become overrun with decadence. Aunt Sally was a shrewd businesswoman and her business was prostitution. She garnered the wealthiest and most indulgent people of the time and they all found refuge at the House of Pearl.

Prima was now a blossoming young lady of fifteen, she was bright and beautiful, and had learned to live with the demons of the home and her unconventional lifestyle. Prima's job at the house was mostly to run errands for Sally and get things for the working girls.

All of the girls knew about the house and its "possessions," in fact, many of them attributed the ghosts to being a help during particularly "painful" or "deviant" clients. One girl, Lydia, an orphaned and abused girl of nineteen, swore that the spirits helped her and even enhanced her experience with men she didn't particularly care for. They made her want it, and when it was over, she pretended that it was someone else in her body doing those nasty things, not her. It was small, but it was the only consolation she had and it made life bearable for her.

Aunt Sally was a true Madame, and she ran this whorehouse with an iron fist, the girls worked six days a week on rotation, and everyone helped out with the chores, although Prima did more housework than the rest. She was a slave in her own home and her innocence and happiness had been taken from her long ago,

there was no room in this young lady's life for love or laughter, just sadness and tears.

⚓

The devilish spirits had learned much over the years and were now able to possess people at will. You never knew where one would come from, and sometimes it would render you in a type of coma, unable to react but free from pain or the discomfort inherent in their business.

On this day, one would be there for Prima for the worst violation imagined: her Aunt Sally was negotiating with an infamous criminal for the virginity of her niece. Even in these times, the late nineteen thirties, the money was obscene, ten thousand dollars for the privilege of having the virgin Pearl. Both would take their cut, and Sally would make a pretty hefty sum on this.

Contract completed, Prima's virginity had been sold to the highest bidder and the deal was about to be consummated. A gangster named "Babyface" Nelson, who was hiding out in Sausalito under the pseudonym Lester Gillis, had the winning bid, and he was on his way to claim his precious prize. Prima had no idea what this day was going to be like for her, but she would be unusually thankful for the numbing presence of the spirits of the house.

As a beige and black 1932 Mercedes Benz Maybach Zeppelin rolled up to the house, inside the luxury sedan sat an impeccably dressed man, but underneath the fine suit you could see the man was bad news, a bad guy with a lot of money. "Babyface" Nelson was a killer and notorious gangster and he was here to claim Prima as the prize of a vile contest orchestrated by Aunt Sally.

Sally was dressed in her finest red gown and looked extra gaudy today as she greeted him with the exuberance of a child opening a Christmas present.

"Mr. Lester Gillis, what an honor. Welcome to the House of Pearl," Sally squealed.

"Sally, I presume," "Babyface" said with a bit of disdain, "Where is she, I have heard so much of her beauty."

"Sir, she is waiting for you in the main parlor," Sally said as she ushered him in and down the long hallway to the luxurious main parlor.

Inside the main parlor, Prima had been called and told to dress in a new gown, made of off-white silk and no undergarments. Her body was young and lithe, and the dress should have been for her wedding night.

The parlor had a large bed in it, with silken linens all white and smelling of lusty fragrances and the ocean. A feast of food, wine, cognac and whisky adorned a buffet table at the far end of the room.

The other girls knew what was about to happen and tried to ease her fears, but Prima was no idiot, and she knew what was about to happen to her. She had thought it would happen someday, but now that it was here, she was terrified.

Prima's makeup was minimal, a bit of blush and a splash of lipstick; there was nothing more that was needed, as she was strikingly beautiful. The girls did well, and she was lovely and desirable, understated and innocently sexy.

"Babyface" walked into the room and looked at Prima and grinned widely, he had a psychotic look about him and it made Prima uneasy.

"Leave us," he ordered to his driver as he shut the door on Sally and the rest of the girls.

Prima was now left alone with one of the most notorious and violent gangsters alive, she looked around, but no one would come and save her. She shivered in the corner as he came closer to her.

"So, you're the girl?"

"Yes, I'm Prima, please sir, don't hurt me. I have never..." She pleaded with him.

"Yes well, someday you will be famous because it was "Babyface" Nelson who broke you, you know who I am don't you?"

"Yes, sir."

"Are you afraid?"

"Yes, sir."

"Well, you should be, let me see your body, take your gown down, not all the way, just your breasts, slowly girl, slowly."

As he watched her, he poured a large glass of brandy for her and motioned for her to drink it. Drink it all. She obliged and instantly felt relaxed and a little light-headed; she didn't drink alcohol so this was another first for her.

As "Babyface" began to touch her, she felt sick and tried to get away from him, but he grabbed her hard, almost bruising her arms.

"You can make this easy or hard, pretty one, I'll get it either way."

Prima looked around, but no one was there, "Babyface" smelled of cologne, cigars, booze and he had bad cigar breath: his foul smell made Prima sick to her stomach. As he began to grope at her and kiss her, she looked around for any distraction, and then she saw it, *her old friend, the ceiling pearl.*

The pearl that made her father crazed and murdered her mother and the same that made him take his life. That pearl that made her an orphan, and now it was making her a whore. She hated it and yet welcomed it, she prayed it would come quickly and take her and make her numb. Maybe she would wake up and it would be all over, like Lydia said, just like nothing ever happened.

The deep violet ceiling began to swirl until a bright white pearlescent sphere appeared in the center. It fell and as it dripped down it landed on her head, she felt awash with a sensation of hunger and debauchery and she swooned at this man's touch. Inside, she was disgusted: but the pearl would let her perform and pretend to be in ecstasy; even if it wasn't really true. "Babyface" groped and grunted, and as he penetrated her over and over again, she drifted off into a drug-like stupor.

Two hours later, leaving her lying there naked, "Babyface" got dressed, took a long swig of brandy, and left without so much as a "thank you" to Prima. He lit a cigar as he bounded out of the parlor, satisfied with his purchase.

Prima sat on the tousled silken bed, surrounded by the bloodstained sheets of what was left of her virtue. Gone now forever, she would never be the same and something cold and heartless switched on for her that night, something that she would never recover from for many years to come.

⚓

As the years went by, Prima had learned the game, and thanks to the ceiling pearls, life was almost bearable. How strange that it was her dire enemy and yet her savior. She had no desire to reconcile these thoughts of the pearl as her heart was now numb to the pleasures and pain of her taxing work as a prostitute.

Prima spent most days with clients and in time she became the most desired of all of Sally's girls, with the help of her ceiling pearls, she was able to do what Lydia had done, pretend it was another person and that it would all be alright someday.

It was during these years that she had become pregnant by a client, and while she was in the last month of the pregnancy, Sally sequestered her away from prying eyes.

Prima gave birth to a bright eyed, dark-haired baby girl late one stormy evening, only Sally and a midwife who Prima had never seen were in attendance. Prima was so deadened to life and emotions now that she didn't even want to hold the baby girl or noticed that they had taken a picture. Prima woke hours later; no one was in the room. The bloody sheets were changed, Prima was washed and in a fresh nightgown, and the newborn baby was nowhere to be found.

Nothing was ever said again about the fate of the little baby who came and went so quietly in the night.

Five years had passed since the baby, and for the cold-hearted Prima, life was like a wheel that she went round and round on. She smoked opium during the day and drank late at night to sleep, and in between, the ceiling pearls appeared when the men came.

One day the entire house was abuzz with the arrival of a new set of clients, Hollywood types, and movie stars to boot. And the main man was Stanley Payden, thought by many to be the most beautiful man in the movies, and he was coming to Sally's! The girls were all hoping to be with him, but as usual, like all the rest, he saw only Prima when they lined up for approval.

She went into the large parlor with Stanley behind her: looking at her, he was immediately taken by her beauty. He was also bothered by her detachment and he wanted to talk before business.

As Prima looked at him, she offered him a drink and he smiled graciously, she looked at him and saw something different in him, he was kind and self-assured, and he was smitten with Prima.

"Prima, what a lovely name," Stanley said trying to make conversation.

"I don't know where it came from, my parents died when I was very young," she said taken back by her openness with this man.

As she sat with Stanley, they talked until late that evening, she told him everything, and for the first time in years, the pearl didn't come, it wasn't there. It was just Prima and Stanley. She told him of her father's suicide after murdering her mother, of Aunt Sally showing up, selling her virginity, the baby.... *everything, absolutely everything.*

As they talked, Stanley had already begun to make a plan, one that Prima would find out about in a few months. Stanley fell in love with her that night and vowed to make things right for her, no matter how much it cost or who he had to walk over to get it done. He was rich, powerful, and famous, and he was going to make sure that he would right the wrongs that had been done to Prima.

As the months passed, they got closer, but Prima never really let him in totally after that first night. At this point in her life, it was just a good thing that she didn't hate him, so she was essentially making baby strides back to normality. For now, she was still very detached.

"I found her, your baby," Stanley blurted out one night.

"What?"

"I found your baby girl, Sally and that midwife witch, gave her to an orphanage while you were sleeping and paid them off to say nothing. My P.I. found her."

"Your what?"

"P.I., Private Investigator. I wanted to find her for you."

"No, I couldn't be any kind of mother to her. Can you find a good home for her though, give her money."

"Of course, Prima, but are you sure?"

"Yes, I have no love to give a child and I certainly don't know how to be a mother. But can you do me one favor with respect to her, call her Peaks?"

"Sure, but what does that mean?"

"When she was born, I thought she would have so many challenges, mountains—peaks to climb. So that was the name I wanted for her, when I think of her I call her Peaks."

"Of course, but there's one other thing, about your Aunt Sally."

"What?"

"Well, she's really not your Aunt, she's been pretending all these years and planned to run your estate to the ground. Use you to fund her brothels."

"Oh God, Stanley..."

"Well, I've taken care of that too... Any minute now."

Just as Stanley said this, Prima could hear sirens winding through the curvy streets of Sausalito. She ran to the window and looked out: a Sausalito Police Department Paddy wagon was pulling up and three more police cars followed, it was a raid!!!

Suddenly all hell broke loose in the house, naked girls ran everywhere, police ran in and arrested everyone, everyone but Prima.

An imposing cop named Sergeant Flaherty looked at Sally with disgust, "Mizz Emeral, you're under arrest Ma'am, for stealing from the estate of one Prima Pearl, of prostitution, drug dealing, pandering, gambling, and that's just the beginning."

Sally tried to object, but in a flash she was gone, along with everyone else in the house. Prima stood there unable to move, she tried to process what had just happened.

A team of locksmiths stood at the bottom of the broad wooden staircase that led to the front door, waiting for the fracas to die down. Once everyone had left, Stanley's crew marched up the front stairs of the house and stood by Stanley as he and Prima were left alone in the house: Stanley stood there like he was the Sergeant at Arms.

"Go to town boys, button the place down, nobody in here that Miss Pearl here doesn't approve of. Got it?"

"Yes Sir!" they cried in unison.

With military precision the locksmiths pulled all the locks off all exterior doors and secured the windows, no one would get in here after tonight.

"Stanley, but how?" she was stunned.

"Well, being rich and famous has it perks you know." He said smugly.

"Thank you, Stanley, thank you," Prima hugged him as she looked about the house that was now all hers.

⚓

Some days later.

Prima looked out the windows of the limo, and smiled. She had decided to leave and as Sausalito and San Francisco faded away and the planes of the airport became larger and larger, she felt a great release of her burden. Prima was packed and ready for an international adventure, time to get away from the sadness and past tragedies that surrounded the house. Stanley's team of shrewd lawyers had been able to regain all of Prima's family holdings, and even though Sally was a crook, she had made quite a bit of money for the Pearl Estate, and Prima was a very, very wealthy young woman. Since it was all originally in a trust for Prima, it had matured and Prima had tens of millions at her disposal.

She took Stanley's lawyer's advice and let them administer the funds, there would be no checkbook balancing for Prima. A good international bank would do the lawyer's bidding and she could have anything she wanted and held letters of credit for every bank in the world from Argentina to Timbuktu. Finally she was free and no one could ever tell her what to do again.

The lawyers also created and managed a trust for Peaks, who was now adopted by a wealthy couple in Tiburon who were unable to have children. They doted on her and had no idea that this little orphan was worth ten times more than they were worth, but they loved her and gave her a lovely family life. It made Prima happy to know that, even though her heart was void of intimacy, and the thought of being a mother frightened her.

But here in the car with Stanley, she was sad to say goodbye, and he knew it as well, he cared for her deeply and had helped her get her life back, he knew they would be bonded for life. But he also knew that she had to go, and he was prepared to say goodbye.

The long black limousine pulled up to the baggage check at the Pan Am Airlines Terminal at San Francisco International Airport. SFO was a busy airport and commuters bustled in and out of the terminal. Prima and Stanley climbed out as the valets went for the numerous bags she had brought with her. She was now an heiress on an adventure and had the bags to show for it.

"Good bye, Prima, I'll always love you."

"I know Stanley, thank you for everything, really... I don't know how I can ever thank you."

"You just have. Good luck, stay in touch," but deep down inside he knew she wouldn't and that she was gone, cut off from him forever.

They hugged tightly as two lovers who knew this was their last moment together; it was bittersweet for both of them, as they knew Prima was off to better places and leaving the sadness of her childhood behind her.

She waved goodbye to Stanley and wondered if she would ever see him again. But she had her life back, she had money and now, no one would ever, ever tell her what to do, where to go or who to be with. No one would ever get close to her again, that way she would be protected, never let anyone in again, never love, never get hurt.

Chapter 13

Elia took another sip of wine, and settled down to tell Paul more.

"She sounds like she was really messed up, I don't know if I could ever recover from that. Where did she go? What did she do?" Paul was like a kid who couldn't wait for the next chapter of his favorite book.

"She left....that was in the early 50's and she lived like a nomad, going from country to country, from boats to trains to ocean-liners. She was beautiful and rich and of course, had many, many friends. Prima had so much money, but from what I know, she didn't want anything to do with the kid, Peaks."

"How could she do that?" Paul asked indignantly.

"I don't really know, but people do stuff sometimes that seems like the right thing to do at the time for their survival."

"You sound like you condone what she did."

"Not at all, but we all have stuff that we're not proud of."

Paul thought for a second about all the women he's toyed with and how many times he's been called out for being a pig, a liar, even a scumbag, the list went on... "Yeah, you've got a point."

"But Prima was a strong woman, and a survivor, you know?"

"No doubt, anyone that didn't end up in the funny farm after that would have to be more than just a survivor."

"Well, she had her challenges, but she was strong, maybe the house helped her a bit, you know, maybe the spirits felt sorry for her and gave her a little something. I don't know."

"Maybe, I guess it's the least they could do after all they took from her." Paul said rather insightfully, it made Elia think.

"I guess I never thought about it like that, but yeah, maybe you're right. Maybe you're right."

Elia started to tell Paul more of Prima's life after the day she was liberated from Sally's whorehouse.

Oddly enough, leaving San Francisco would be the easiest thing that Prima would ever do. Seeing her father murder her mother, having her life derailed by being forced into a brothel by her erstwhile aunt would have made a lesser person go crazy, but not Prima. Maybe it was the closeness she had with the spirit world, but someone helped her be strong and survive this, was it the house? Was it Oshima? Was it something she didn't know yet? What she did know was that she was ready to take charge of her life.

Stanley had been a God-send, his team of attorneys had been particulary adept at getting Prima's life back, financially and personally. The Sausalito District Attorney threw the book at Sally Emeral, and the entire trial was done behind closed doors. This left Prima with a spotless reputation. In fact, even some of the neighbors didn't know what went on in that old house, and that was fine with Prima, and especially the Standishes who felt guilty about leaving her with her fake Aunt Sally.

As she got into the giant Pan Am jet, she went to her first-class seat and was given a glass of Dom Perignon champagne by the picture-perfect blonde-haired, blue-eyed stewardess. Her beauty was not lost on Prima, who thought to herself, *Aunt Sally would kill to have her, too bad that bitch is rotting in jail.*

She laughed at the thought of Sally in prison, toasted her champagne to the former Madame and downed the glass. She sighed heavily.

The perky stewardess passed her with the bottle again, "Miss Pearl, can I give you a refill?"

"Yes, uhm," Prima looked at her name tag, "Penny, yes, I would love another glass, thank you."

As the jet taxied to the runway, this would be the beginning of years of travel and a new life for Prima. Her old life was behind her now, forever...... and a new, glamorous one was within her reach.

Prima was presented as a young heiress who was just coming into her fortune and introduced to the wealthy and elite of San Francisco Society before she left. Wherever she travelled from then on, she would be received by the best families and was a sought after lady in every city around the world.

She sat front row at the Chanel fashion shows in Paris, attended polo matches in Buenos Aires, Argentina, was front and center at Teatro La Scala in Milan, and costume parties in the canal mansions of Venezia. She even partied in London at some skinny rocker's house named Mick Jagger, she thought his band was pretty good. Everywhere she travelled to, she was with the young and hip crowd, and there were parties twelve months of the year.

She was beautiful, young and rich, and sought after for her quick acerbic wit and was always the life of the party.

As the years had passed, Prima began to feel calm about life and felt the pangs of home calling her. It was the nineteen sixty's and she finally felt ready to see it again, the house.... The House of Pearl, uncertain if she was ready to experience it again.

As she arrived in San Francisco, she remembered how beautiful the city was, the architecture, the landscape, the people, everything. As her limousine pulled up to the airport curb and she climbed in, she asked the driver to tour her around the city, she had read so many articles about the Hippie movement and the music and social scene in the Haight-Ashbury District that she wanted to see it for herself.

It was amazing, hundreds of people living communally in the streets and apartments of this area, music played, marijuana was being smoked, and everyone seemed high as kites from taking LSD and other drugs of choice.

Prima rolled down the window of the limo to take in the smells and sights: she loved this.

A young woman, dressed in paisley, messed up hair with ribbons and flowers tied up in it, looked at the limo and waved.

"Driver, stop the car please," Prima yelled.

The car screeched to a stop and Prima stuck her head out the window, the young woman looked at her, this was the Haight, and anything could happen here.

"Well, hello rich lady," the raspy-voiced woman said.

"The name's Prima, Prima Pearl," Prima said kindly.

"Janis, Janis Joplin, and I'm a singer." The woman said somewhat stoned and woozy.

"Nice to meet you, Janis the singer," Pearl said seriously.

"Whoa, Pearl, lordy Pearl, won't you buy me a Mercedes Benz, Sam honey look at what we're gonna be ride'n in, after everybody knows us." She heard a young and very green Janis Joplin sing in her raspy and hypnotic voice right there in the infamous Haight-Ashbury District of San Francisco.

Prima invited her into the car and Janis obliged and directed her to a party where some of her friends were hanging out.

Everyone was there, Jimi Hendrix, her old friend Mick Jagger, even the Mamas and the Papas: Prima was part of a very chic party scene, and being so rich and lovely, everyone wanted to be her friend. She had many acquaintances, but never once did she let anyone get close to her.

After weeks of hanging out and staying at the best hotels in the city, Prima thought it was time to say goodbye to her new party friends, but she vowed to stay in touch. She said her goodbyes to Janis and the ladies hugged like old friends, the rich heiress and budding songstress.

"Goodbye my friend, come by my place in Sausalito when you get some time, and please, bring everyone over." Pearl said back then and handed Janis a card, she liked their musical talent.

"Pearl, ah? That's a cool name. I always liked it, you know? Mind if I borrow it?" Janis replied to her as she drove away in her limousine.

They would come by the place in Sausalito many times and have many parties there; it was a special time for Pearl and her hippie friends.

Pearl remembered fondly the wild times they had when they stayed with her at the house. And she was still mad at Janis for stealing her name, Pearl..... *Oh well, let bygones be bygones, right?*

⚓

After spending a few months with her new hippie friends, Pearl decided to call Stanley and meet with him. Surely he knew she was in town and was wanting to see her, she felt happy to see him, but she wasn't the same as the young girl who left here so many years ago.

What she felt for Stanley was something, but she was sure

it wasn't love, whatever it was, she was grateful to him for his loyalty and friendship, and they would always remain close.

By the time they set up a lunch date, she was resolved that she would be leaving again soon, her wanderlust had kicked in and she was ready to say hi and goodbye at the same sitting.

As she waited for him at D' Oros, a fabulous Italian restaurant in the city, she thought of what her life might be like if she had stayed here. The air smelled of fresh bread and garlic and delicious food, it was comforting to be here. The restaurant made her love the city and the grand eatery was as opulent and classy as San Francisco always felt to her. But she couldn't stay and wanted to tell Stanley that in person.

As she sipped a glass of Italian Asti Spumante, Stanley sauntered into the large ornate room, handsome, sun-bleached and self-assured, she smiled at him. He grinned widely at the sight of her.

"God, Prima, you look better than ever, you look beautiful," he said sincerely and excitedly.

"Hi Stanley."

"I hear you've been tearing up the town here, young lady."

"Whatever could you mean, my dear?" as she said this, she stood up to greet him and he grabbed her and hugged her tightly, it was wonderful for him, but awkward for her, and Stanley drew back a little bit.

He could see that the distance was still there between them, and although he had hoped for more out of this meeting, it was clear that they would leave as friends and nothing more. He was disappointed but not surprised.

"Well then, tell me what's been going on," he said as he tried to divert the attention from his wounded psyche to her adventures.

They talked for what seemed like hours, many courses and coffees and drinks, and finally dessert. They talked of Stanley's sea adventures, his movies, his kids, his divorces, her men, and they laughed for long periods of time. *It was good to see him,* she thought.

Their time together was coming to a close and they had a bit of business to discuss.

"So, where is she?" Prima finally blurted out.

"What?" Stanley asked.

"You know, the kid, where is she?"

"Oh, well, she's just finishing high school, she's very bright and got into Stanford, a bit of a braniac. She wants to be a photo jounalist."

"Oh," Prima said sadly.

"Do you want to see her now, after all these years? She doesn't really know anything about you."

"No, I, I don't know."

"That's what you wanted, right?"

"Yes, of course. It's just..."

"You can't have it both ways, you know. I did what you asked me and you can't take that back now, she's happy and has a great life. You're not going to screw that up are you?" Stanley said somewhat angrily.

"Of course not, no. I did the right thing, I just wanted to know that she was OK, I guess."

"Yes, she's great."

"Well then, I guess I'm happy."

"So, Prima Pearl, lady of the world, where are you off to now?" Stanley quickly changed the subject.

"India, I think. I was invited to a party for the Maharasha of Delhi and thought some time travelling around there would be good for me, maybe find some kind of peace, you know." She said, and forced a smile.

"Maybe so, Prima, I hope you find it, I know things weren't the best for you growing up, so I do hope you find what you're looking for. I hope you find happiness. I mean it." Stanley said, his eyes clouded up a bit at the realization that they were about to say goodbye.

"I'm trying Stanley, I'm trying," Prima said, getting a bit choked up as well.

"Stay in touch, Okay?"

"Of course, thank you Stanley, for everything.."

They hugged goodbye and Stanley got up to leave.

"Oh, and you've got the check right?" he smiled sarcastically at her.

"Yes, Mister Big-Shot Movie Star, I've got this." She smiled, glad that their last exchange would be a good laugh.

Stanley left the restaurant, and as he walked out the door Prima knew deep down that this would be the last time they saw each other. He was the last anchor she had here and now she was free again and off to another adventure.

Her limousine pulled up outside the restaurant, ready to take her to the airport, and far, far away again from the House of Pearl and those she left behind.

Chapter 14

$\mathcal{A}$s Paul stood looking at Elia, he was amazed at the story of Prima.

"So, what else, did she break Stanley's heart again?" He sincerely felt sorry for Stanley. "How could she, after all he did for her?"

"It was the 60's, they were wild times."

"But that didn't excuse what she did."

"True, but the real shocker came when she came back here, to meet me."

"Wa-, wa, wait, you guys have met?"

"Oh yeah, settle in for this one." Elia began the long tale of Prima's journey back to the house after many years.

"After my parents were killed in the car accident, there was a lot of weird stuff that went on. I found out that I didn't really have any other family, but some lawyers had arranged for me to be a ward of an old family friend."

"*Stanley?*"

"Of course, seems like that's the story of my family, sadness... but Stanley was a kind old man."

"So, you knew him too, wow, how did that happen?"

"I'll get to that, Paul, now let me finish will you?"

⚓

Prima Pearl moved around India from ashram to princely palaces taking in as much as she could of the ancient culture. India was in a new day and something extraordinary was arising. Unbeknownst to me, what was to be my grandmother was sent on a journey to meet me. She was descended from a niece who inherited the house from Edwin, although it was unclear if she ever lived there. Ultimately, it was passed down to Prima's mother who did move in with her father after many years of being abandoned.

Years had passed and a 70-year old, Prima Pearl now lived on a well-appointed houseboat on Lake Dahl in Srinagar, Kashmir part of Northern India. As she sat in her floating luxury home, the seventy-year old Prima Pearl felt something was wrong. She was a wealthy and connected great old lady now, and she had a longing for her family and the house she left so many years ago. *But why*, she would think to herself, it had caused so much grief, why did she even think about it at all?

She was halfway around the world, and it still occupied her thoughts.

She had lost her parents from her father being possessed by the ghost that made him strangle her mother, and then he shot himself in the head from his maddening grief of his crazed action. Prima had left that house behind and had lived for so many years in India and lived a clean life, no drugs and no drinking to excess. Her skin was slightly wrinkled for her age, yet she looked much younger than seventy and her eyes showed the wisdom of a world traveler, as did her wardrobe.

Prima was searching through her old keepsakes with her dearest friend. Nitya was an Indian woman who resided in the houseboat with her. These two women had been friends for years. In their large houseboat filled with rare antiquities and fine furniture, they lived a happy and quiet life.

"I didn't know you had one of those magic boxes. My family's factory made those in Madras, back in the late nineteenth century, so many years ago, they're collectable now, Pearl."

"Yes Nitya, my mother, bless her heart, found it in the old house we moved into, when I was still a baby. She gave it to me on my tenth birthday. It's held a lot of memories for me over the years."

Nitya looked at the box with Prima. Nitya picked it up out of her friend's hands and fumbled with it.

"So tell me Pearl, what long hidden secret did you put in the secret compartment, some naked pictures of an old lover, a gold coin, huh, let's see."

To Prima's surprise, Nitya opened the secret compartment and out fell a wedding picture of Oshima from 1888. In the picture she was holding the keepsake box standing next to Captain Edwin who is brandishing a samurai sword, and she was surrounded by all of her family members back in Japan. Also in the drawer next to the picture was a small key.

"I never knew about that drawer. Let me see that. Don't drop the key!"

"Hey look there's a little book hidden in here. I think it's, yes it's, it's a little diary."

"Let me see that Nitya! I suppose the little key fits in here, yep, well look at this."

Pearl took the little diary and looked at it curiously with expectations. She opened it randomly to any page and realized that it was written in Japanese.

"It's in Japanese, it must be Japanese because Oshima was Japanese."

"Let me translate that for you. You start packing and I'll have the translation ready for you before you leave. Let me read a little bit right now for you."

133

The small old diary was translated by Nitya and read as follows:

> ...but I didn't count on his incredibly sensitive eyes, and the power of his embrace. My shipboard dalliance with the young officer was meaningless as soon as my eyes saw his wise old seasoned eyes again.
>
> I've arrived here in California to live with this man of the sea, and my family is pleased, and that makes me happy, but I am not always tickled, for he will be away at sea for long periods of time, and I have been miserable during these absences. There have been reports of marauding pirates up and down the coast. I can only hope they don't enter the bay. I am too close to the gate and would be easy prey. I'm truly afraid. I don't believe that I will live long like this, I miss my family, and I'm afraid...

Prima was shocked to have found this and now and to hear the translation. "Wow! I need to slow down and take a breath. This is all too much too fast. Don't you think so, Nitya?"

"Well, it's exciting, that's for sure. Let's keep going."

"No, why don't you take this, and do your translation? I'd like to stop for a moment and meditate on this." Prima said as Nitya sat at the desk and began writing.

Except for the scribbling of her pen, outside the sounds of birds began to chirp and children played in the water: it was a peaceful morning. Then the phone rang, and it's an overseas call for Prima Pearl.

"Now what, what more can happen today? Pearl says answering the telephone. Yes, Pearl here."

"Pearl Arnold?

"Yes this is Pearl Arnold." She replied as she sometimes went by the name of her last, late husband.

"Prima Pearl Arnold?"

"God, it's so amazing, calling from half-way around the world, I swear, it sounds like you're standing right next to me."

"Rose, is that you? Hold on let me sit down. Good lord, how are you? Can you hear me?"

"Yes I hear you great."

"Why are you calling? Is something wrong with the house, with you, or your family?"

On the other end was Rose Standish, her old friend and neighbor, "I can't believe I have finally found you! Oh, Prima, It has taken me so long; I have had detectives and consulates looking for you. You are one hard lady to locate."

"India is an easy place to get lost in, my old friend. So to what do I owe the honor of your call?"

"Well yes, it's the house, that guy who moved in last summer, he died yesterday, in the house."

"No!" She turned to Nitya shocked who was still translating the diary.

"Yes."

"Well, I am truly saddened by this. Why are you calling, to tell me this?" Prima seemed annoyed, but she knows it's important for her.

"It's so complicated I just wish you could be here. Remember Stanley? He has been renting the house for the last few years. Well, apparently he was caretaking a fifteen year-old daughter of a friend who had died suddenly. At any rate, he's dead now too, it's all too much for me Pearl, I just manage family estates now and a few houses, please come home. Just for a little while."

"Stanley, what are you talking about?"

"See, I told you it was complicated."

"I don't understand."

"Oh, and the girl's name is the same as yours, it's Pearl... Pearl, are you there? I said her name is *Pearl*."

"Rose, darling... what?? You say that there is another Pearl in that house, and Stanley was living there? I have to meet this girl," Prima strained to listen to the other end.

"Alright, Rosie, yes of course, I'll come as soon as I can get a flight."

The phone line started to crackle and faded in and out, and then they lost reception.

Prima hung up the phone and turned to Nitya and blurted out, in utmost surprise, the news of another Pearl staying in her home and what a coincidence it was. They both sat and chatted about how it may not be a coincidence but fate. Hurriedly, they booked Pearl the earliest flight to San Francisco.

This visit was going to bring about more than either of them knew and possibly answers to the supernatural possession of this house.

⚓

Prima Pearl was up for the day earlier than usual. She skipped her breakfast and reading the paper which was her usual leisurely morning. Then in haste she ordered a taxi to get her to the train on time to catch her flight. She pondered what was ahead of her and she was totally intrigued at the occurrence of a girl named Pearl in her childhood home.

It would take her a full day to get to a train that would take her to the airport in Delhi, and then another thirty hours on three different flights to get to San Francisco, but this she felt was a journey she needed to undertake. She left her life of meditation and serenity which was not something she had thought of doing for many years, but the house beckoned and she would heed its call.

The airport was busy. Flights were arriving and leaving and the mood was one of, on the go! Over the speakers Pearl heard that her flight would be departing on time and would all passengers please proceed through to the flight gates. Gate 608 was ready and the passengers slowly entered the massive two story jet liner.

Pearl was sitting in First Class on Pan Am round the world flight 001. A long haul multiple layover flight to San Francisco. She settled into her seat and looked out the window as the plane took off. Prima meditated. She wanted to be at ease with whatever this long flight had ahead of her.

The plane had been flying for some time and she decided to look again at the little diary they had found in the box. She began to read Nitya's typed translations.

The plane had reached cruising altitude and the seat belt signs were off and people moved about the cabins, went to the bathrooms, and stretched.

The flight attendant served and chatted with the first class passengers and she neared Prima.

"Would you like anything? I brought you an extra blanket just in case it gets too cold for you."

Pearl looked at the Flight Attendant it was the same young blue eyed girl from so many years ago, just a little thicker but just as pleasant, and she put down her diary translations.

"Oh yes, thank you dear." Pearl replied and settled back into the drone of the jet engines and read her little diary.

Pearl found herself reminiscing about her time living in the Sausalito house, when she had returned in the sixties. Then she was younger and eager to find the house standing even in need of repair. She remembered the sixties free love era and she smiled.

She recalled a person asking for money while others sung of *free love*. She smirked mockingly thinking...*free love...it's never free*. Her exact same thoughts back then, when she had leaned out of her limousine and grabbed the guitar off a hippie band, and began playing her own set of music to the crowd's liking. Back then she even got money given to her and her adopted hippie band by the crowd. None of them ever realized how rich she was.

Pearl looked again out of the plane's window, she reflected on that amazing moment when she met Janis Joplin, who became a world-renowned music legend! Pearl had met Janis before her great rise to fame. She recalled their conversation word for word...

⚓

The hours proceeded forward and it was now landing time for her flight. Pearl exited the plane with vigor to go seek this young woman in her home.

It felt like the limousine ride was never-ending, and then her eyes cast onto the house she hadn't seen in twenty years. She remembered its appeal and its craziness, as she waved to Rose the realtor, who had phoned her the other day. Her childhood friend Rosie, the little girl who waved goodbye; now after many years of travels and life, they were together again and old ladies. How befitting Prima thought.

Standing near Rose was a young woman of fifteen who was the ward of Stanley's, the man that once loved Prima and who had recently died.

The young lady, Elia, was nervous and excited by what Rose told her about this seventy year old woman, maybe she could get more answers about this house or in finding her family.

The House of Pearl

"Pearl, I want you to meet, Pearl. Elia Pearl." Rose said patting Elia on her shoulder.

"My goodness... Pearl, your name really is Pearl? What an odd circumstance. When Rose told me your name, I said to my friend, that I had to return, just to meet you."

The three women walked slowly into the house as Elia spoke.

"I thought I was the only Pearl these days as it's not a popular modern name, apparently also it was a name that Stanley fancied and he was friends with my mom and dad. Stanley would sometimes yell out my name when he was sick and delusional, it was like he knew somebody named Pearl from his past."

Prima Pearl listened very interested in what this girl had to say; she had a long history with Stanley and was shocked to see that he had been living in the house and such a big part of this girl's life. *But why?*

The three women moved into the Dining Room.

Prima and Rose hugged, almost like they were kids again, and as they broke their embrace, they smiled at each other, both thought after all these years how nice it was to be together again.

"Well my dear, maybe this is some form of serendipity. Rose, I can take it from here, thanks so much, I'll call you tomorrow." Prima said as she sat on a large cushioned chair.

"Sure Prima, we'll talk later. Bye, little Pearl." Rose walked out and went onto her next client.

"It's funny, you remind me... of me. You almost look like what I looked like, except for the clothes, but we had more fashion sense back then. I met a boy here, in this house, like you I was very young at the time, and my parents had just died."

"Prima, really, your parents died too?"

"Yes child, and I was completely destroyed, and know something of what you must feel right now. I'm thinking I can help you through this my dear. Back then my so-called Aunt Sally came to live with me. I thought that this young man whom I thought I loved, would return, but he never did. He destroyed something inside of me; I even got pregnant and gave up the baby without a care, well, sort of. Boy, you sure are stirring up a lot of old stuff I haven't thought about for a long, long time." Prima went off to a memory that made her very, very sad.

Elia just watched and listened, she felt eased to hear that someone else, had felt her emotions before, and what she had been through.

Elia questioned "So who was Stanley to you and how did you meet him? And why have we been brought together here. Who are you?" Elia had more questions than answers and it overwhelmed Prima.

"First thing's first. Let me show you something Elia." Pearl retrieved her old keepsake box from one of her bags and continued, "I was so angry, sad, and disillusioned with life. And Stanley saved me; I never really loved again after Stanley. He was tall and strong and he had such a deep resonant voice that mesmerized my heart."

"Did you ever see any of Stanley's movies?" Elia asked.

"No Elia, I didn't really know much about him, he was just my friend, and someone I loved. He loved me too. I don't see too many movies anyway; I just never had the time."

"Here these are the letters that Stanley had returned to him. I never had the heart to throw them out."

Prima looked at these letters; she was intrigued by what Elia was sharing. Prima's eyes caught something unusual about these letters. They were addressed to Prima Pearl, and some came from the house on Bridgeway.

Tears formed in Prima's eyes, this was something she had not allowed herself to do or feel for decades. To remember her lost loves made her vulnerable and remorseful.

"If I had only known he was here, for those years, I had my early love living in the same house that we met in. God, this beautiful house, has tormented me so, I could have come back here so easily." Prima said with tears in her eyes, of the loss of this man.

"He used to yell out my name before he died, yell out Pearl, and really yell it out. And when I would come to him, he would swear I wasn't Pearl, and I thought it was just his medication causing him to hallucinate, but maybe he was being tormented by the house spirit making him relive in his mind, old experiences with you, that he couldn't hold onto when he was awake."

"Did you just say house spirit?" Prima Pearl asked, knowing about this house's ghostliness.

"Yeah, I swear this house is haunted, in fact I have evidence, kind of." Elia went to a box she had and opened it to reveal a collection of pearls. "I've been collecting these from around the house sometimes they fall on me, when they do, I have a sudden warm rush throughout my body. Sometimes they just drop and don't do anything. They looked pretty real so I've been collecting them."

They stared at each other.

"Yes honey, I've walked these steps before you."

"I don't believe it! You too, Prima?"

"I know that this house is haunted by some... thing I've seen it. I think it had something to do with my parents' death."

"Really?"

"Oh my, you don't know anything about me do you, Elia. Come here give me a big hug."

"Thanks I think I really needed that."

"We all do Elia, at all ages. I found this diary that might help us figure this out."

"Tell me more, about you?"

"Elia... that would probably require many hours. Let me tell you a little bit about this house first, we were in it for about fifteen years or so, when my parents, whose love for each other was beginning to blossom again, when my father strangled my mother and shot himself."

"Oh my God! Oh, Oh, I'm so sorry, Prima!"

"I was in the hallway outside the door and I saw something come from the ceiling and remove what appeared to be a partially visible human-like form, which was inside my father... possessing him."

"Yes! Exactly! I've seen that paranormal thing, swimming on the ceiling and coming closer," Elia was shocked at her kinship with Prima.

"Then you know what I'm talking about. After they died, my Aunt Sally came out from St. Louis to help me. She was unique, Sally... ah umm, in the end she wasn't even my Aunt, well, she decided to turn this house into a bordello, it seemed to come awfully easy to her, and it wasn't too out of the ordinary for her. That's when I met Stanley and he later saved my life in a lot of ways."

"It was the ghosts, wasn't it?"

"Yes Elia, you're right. It wasn't until later that we figured the house spirit probably encouraged us to do it. Loveless sex was okay, but real love was too dangerous. The thing got mad, and attacked any show of real love. That's what happened to my parents. I could fake love when I needed to, and I didn't care. And that's why I left; I couldn't live here anymore with it controlling my life and emotions. I couldn't take it if anyone I loved was hurt again. But now, because of you, I'm beginning to care again."

"That's good, right?"

"Elia, not really because, I did one thing in my life that I now regret. I had a baby girl when I was eighteen; very quickly I realized I couldn't keep her. She was taken from me in the night by my Aunt and some evil witchdoctor kind of midwife, when we found her, I named her Peaks, because I knew she would have huge mountains to climb by not having her biological mother around."

Elia heard the name Peaks and nearly fell out of her chair because her mother's name was Peaks and her mother was also adopted. Now these two women's similarities were coming together and their faces and their voices took on new meaning.

"Pearl, my mother's name was, I can't believe this, her name was... Peaks."

"There aren't a lot of women named Peaks."

"Excuse me Elia, did you just tell me that your mother's name was Peaks? Do you have any old baby photos of her?"

"Let me see." Elia said getting up in shock and pleasure at this impossible find. She pulled a photo out.

"Aha, here, yes, this is a good one, she always loved this shot of her, but she never knew where it was shot." Elia Pearl extended the picture of her mother Peaks to Prima. It's a very early baby picture of Peaks, it seemed taken prior to her adoption: a picture that someone took the day of her birth, and took at the bordello. When she held this photo in her hands, Prima Pearl could not control her tears and her eyes welled up and she cried.

"Oh my child, this is truly a miracle! This old lady is going to have her prayers answered. They took this picture when she was only hours old, they sent the picture with her when they gave her up... I am, just, over whelmed, that so many years later Stanley, and my newly discovered granddaughter, have been here all along."

"Did you just call me your granddaughter? "

The two embraced again, both were in tears. They sat together with shock and happiness as they chatted about their likes and dislikes and realized they both shared an ability with music.

As they talked and reminisced, Prima told her how Stanley found the baby, arranged for the adoption, found out about Aunt Sally, and got her out of the house for good.

After a long time, they relaxed and Prima saw that Elia had two guitars in the corner. They both loved music, of course, this was her granddaughter, and they were very much alike.

The house had finally repaid some justice from its supernatural murdering craziness, but was this just the calm before the storm, was the house really pleased with this?

The evening continued and they chatted and bonded over music, dinner and stories.

Chapter 15

The sun was not out today in Sausalito and the overcast sky seemed to suit what Pearl and Elia had decided to do. After a long night of getting to know each other, they came to a conclusion about the fate of the house.

They had decided that today they would have a séance and get rid of the ghost or ghosts that were left, they both had had enough and believed something had to be done and now together they felt strong enough together to do this. The clairvoyant had arrived and they were setting up what was required and told her what had happened in this old house.

"Let's bring that chair over here, great, you sit here, and you here. Now let's concentrate on one thing." The clairvoyant said, with a creepy presence of her own identity. "To sense a spirit let alone get it to cross over, we need time, now sit and allow me to do my job."

"Elia, Are you okay with this?" Prima inquired.

"Sort of, I didn't think she would be this spooky. It's not exactly what you've been describing to me. I'm not sure this spirit likes us. Will it do anything to hurt us?" Elia said now more fearful.

"Shh... I've been able to touch another plane of existence when I am in deep meditation. I can see that you've removed all of the small objects in the room, that usually is sufficient to protect us from the occasionally animated ashtray. Now let's be quiet. Hand me the keepsake box that you know belonged to the spirit we are trying to contact, and give me the box of pearls."

Prima Pearl handed her the keepsake box, and Elia handed her the pearls, she opened the keepsake box to find the photo, the diary, and a pile of pearls.

"Oh my, more pearls, I'm going to put them under this scarf we have in the center of the table."

The room was hazy from the burning incense, and seemed quiet while the ceiling entity quietly and creepily arrived and circled around the chandelier, faster and faster, until the ceiling started to spin like a tornado spiral.

The energy in the room felt crazed and frantic! The ghost seemed out of control and spun around and then suddenly came down and entered the body of the psychic.

"Oh my! She's very strong and very angry, I'm not sure I should take this one on... she seems to want to hurt!" But before she can stop being fully possessed, Oshima locked in and took full control of her body. As Oshima spoke, the pearls under the scarf became agitated and lifted the scarf up until it took the shape of a young Oshima's head, a few pearls flew out and came back like a knife and cut the throat of the apparition. The scarf head tilted and dropped and the pearls flew out from under the scarf one by one. These loose pearls began to circle around the table over their heads.

The spirit began to speak with two voices:

"Hi girls, you are looking good tonight Pearl,
for an old bag, where have you been? I've missed tormenting you,
and who's this irritating young child that resists me?
You're so lovely! How nice!
Three Pearls in one room, and you two, such avid collectors,
I'm impressed.

Thank you for protecting my keepsake box,
the one you've been collecting in, I see you found my diary, tragic,
wasn't it? Soon girls, we'll have a necklace again.
It will be like the pretty one that
I had, when I was a young happily married woman, so many years
ago,
but that evil bastard used it to strangle me,
when he didn't get his way."

The pearls were forming into a necklace over the psychic's head and as little energy sources they began shocking the psychic; she shook a bit at each of the shocks.

"Why are you here in this house? Why won't you go, wherever it is, you're supposed to go?" Prima Pearl asked, she needed answers.

The spirit answered:

"I can't leave! That stupid pirate bastard, boxed me,
and stuffed me away in the attic like some old bottle of rum,
and I was just 26 years old! By the time I figured
out that I was dead, and stuck in this house,
my wonderful husband had already died. Then that miserable imbecile
who cut my throat kept trying to haunt my
house, can you believe that? So I had to spend time and energy keeping
his soul trapped, so that it wouldn't disturb the tenants,
and as long as no one showed any love in the house I didn't care, but
when they did, I would let that miserable freak, break free, and then
someone always died, that's what happened to your parents Prima.
For many years they didn't show any love, so there was nothing
to protect, but then I guess as you got older they found love again and
one day when I wasn't paying attention the spirit of that slowwitted
pirate bastard got out and killed your parents. I'm sorry. Ahhhhh..!
Sorry, I just, I just get so angry sometimes!
That's when I let the other one out of his crypt. Now me, I'm really a

147

sweetheart, you know that Pearl. Remember the night the Mayor and
the Senator came over and we tied the two of them to the...'

"We're not here for those old stories, so are you Oshima?" Prima Pearl interrupted, she just wanted answers to end this!

"Yes my name was Oshima, but Edwin'san called me his Pearl,
his precious Pearl.
If someone would just pay attention and take pity on me, and find my
body, in order to properly bury it in sanctified soil, I could leave
this place. I was so happy coming here as a young woman. My family
was happy and I had money in my pocket, and a solid future, in a
new and exciting city. On the voyage here, I was distracted by a
young dashing lieutenant, who thought he loved me.
I loved his attention, and I was so sad when I arrived in San Francisco.
Maybe that's why I'm being punished. But after I saw the Captain's
incredible eyes again I forgot about the
voyage and became absolutely devoted to Edwin-san, my captain.
Then those damn pirates ruined everything!"

A last large spark crackled in the room and the pearls dropped back down on the table and the house shuttered. Then there was silence.

"She's gone? Tell me, what happened?" the clairvoyant asked, now not possessed by Oshima.

"Yes it seems she has," Elia replied looking around, slightly nervous.

"She told us that we needed to find her body and bury it, to end her supernatural presence here."

"Prima you must do this, the sooner the better. I must leave I'm exhausted, she was angry and strong."

The psychic walked to the door and Elia and Pearl thanked her for her assistance.

"Wow! Pearl we have to get on this!" Elia said walking down the hall to the ladder to the attic and Pearl followed.

They climbed the ladder and entered the attic. It was dusty and full of cobwebs and old artifacts that Elia had not ventured to check ever.

"Oh my!"

"What? Elia?"

"Some of this stuff is beautiful: I can't believe I never came up here before. I suppose I was too scared I might step on the ghost or fall through the ceiling, but now that I have you with me, I feel stronger. Look at this old stuff!"

Prima Pearl saw a golden belt under a trunk; she grabbed one end of it and pulled. This unhinged a group of objects that started to fall. In turn, knocking over a large metal object, which fell and punctured an old crate.

Elia Pearl looked inside the crate and pulled on a few boards, this revealed the mummified body of a young woman. It was the woman in the picture.

It was the corpse of Oshima.

"Pearl, turn around, look what you just did. I think we just found..."

"Oh, oh, I'd say we've found Oshima!"

A ghostly image of the young woman rises out of the old crate and dives away into the floor of the attic.

"Did you just see that?"

"Oh yes Elia, just like the old days, except now I know what to do. We need to bury this body and end this Elia!"

Pearl and Elia planned how this was to be done that day. Together they buried Oshima in the backyard, facing the sea and next to the grave of her beloved Edwin. It took a long time and a great effort for the two women to bury her, but both Prima and Elia knew that if they called the police, there would be even more attention and questions asked. They wanted to avoid all of that and lay poor Oshima to rest. This was the best way.

"She would have liked that, you know." Prima said.

"So do you think this will put to rest the ghosts of the house? And maybe now love can flourish again in this beautiful old home."

"Elia, we can only hope so. You know young lady, I'm feeling pretty good right now, and I have to thank you for that. I hope the two of us become close. I can share some of my experiences with you, so that you don't have to make the same mistakes that I made. I think what I'm saying is, I'd like to welcome you into my family."

"Prima, you're almost like a gift from God, I feel safe again."

The ghost of Oshima was now reunited with the Captain.

Pearl and Elia, walked back up to the house, it seemed Pearl had the ability to unconditionally love again.

After a few weeks together, Prima began to feel as if she needed to get back to her quiet life of solitude in India, back to her friend Nitya and the life she treasured. She loved her granddaughter, and she asked Elia to come back to India with her. Elia wanted to stay in Sausalito, she was young after all and should have the chance to make her own way in life.

Prima and Elia spent their last days together grateful in having been with each other. Elia went on to be a famous singer and Prima would follow her career every bit of the way.

Elia never wanted for anything, and when news of Prima's death reached her, she was inconsolable. Elia heard from Nitya that Prima finally bought a VCR and watched all of Stanley's movies from beginning to end. When she finished the last film, she went to sleep, and her heart just gave out.

Prima died in her 80's quietly in her sleep after a full life. She knew that Elia would be there to carry on the "Pearl" legacy.

It made Elia happy to know that Prima could love after all the time she spent staying away from it, maybe it meant that Elia was bound for true love too.

Chapter 16

$\mathcal{A}$ beautiful day was unfolding and Paul watched Elia as she slept. He knew that he was totally in love with her and this entire process of the house and its weird paranormal occurrences had him wanting to just take her away and escape.

Elia moved around and awoke to see that Paul was watching her.

"Hey," she said as if this were their new morning ritual.

"Hey back to you, Sweetie," Paul kissed her lips, and jumped out of bed "I have to get back to the boat before the owners head off on vacation but, dinner tonight?"

"Sure," Elia replied while sitting up in bed, she watched this handsome man get dressed. "Dinner here?"

"Really?? If I lived in this crazy house I would just leave!" He paused and smiled back at her, "If you need anything today, call me, otherwise I'll see you tonight, dinner, here."

"Did you say the owners are leaving?"

"Yeah, that gives me more time with you, they are off for their usual vacation and I will just stay in port taking care of the yacht until they return. It should be a few months at least."

Paul walked downstairs with Elia behind him on the steps. This unlikely couple seemed to be coming together and their love was beginning to become intense. Paul kissed Elia passionately goodbye. He just wanted to stay with her now and seduce her, but his real day had begun and he had a job to attend to. Elia returned his passion and then watched him walk away, as he waved and rounded the corner towards the marina.

She returned into the house and caught a fleeting shadow dash around the ceiling and some pearls that appeared out of nowhere and seemed to roll around on the floor.

Elia knelt down and looked at the pearls. They seemed real! She looked back up to the ceiling but there was nothing. No apparition, no supernatural beings and she collected the pearls and placed them in a bowl on the coffee table. She walked to her shower and turned the water on and it got steamy.

As the shampoo in her hair flowed down her naked body she wondered why she stayed here, knowing such craziness was possessing this home and she also wondered, why didn't she have any real fear of this place? She felt uncomfortable and confused by it, but she also had an intense fear to run away.

Elia had lost her parents when she was young and had lived with a fake-relative and now, to find some kind of heritage to her background was quite emotional for her. And to now have Paul, her life seemed to change when she was in this house, and she liked it, in spite of the "others" in the house.

Who were her people? Were they here? She knew about them from their history and from her grandmother, but who were they, their souls and their lives? Did they know she was here, were they trying to reach out to her. Why was it easier to live here with the ghosts of her family's past than to be in the real world with the living?

She just needed to know more about her past and this prevailed over any and all of her fears. The house seemed to welcome her and at other times it seemed to push her away, however she held fast and was staying. *No ifs, ands, or ghosts about it.*

Today she had much to do in town and she hurried to get to

the bakery before the homemade fresh bread was sold out. She wanted to treat Paul to it tonight for dinner.

She thought about his eyes, his face and his sensual energy when with her and the passion they shared. Elia knew she was falling for this man. She imagined living with him and the whole family picture was now in her imagination. She dreamed of children with him, and a romance-packed lifestyle with him, she was totally in love with Paul already.

⚓

The sun was out today in Sausalito and Elia drove down the lush roads towards the shops and she could already see the line forming at the bakery. She hurried and stood there too, in line for the best homemade French bread she had ever eaten and seemingly others too. An elderly lady behind her began chatting to her as they were still away from the counter in this queue.

"You are buying the French baguettes dear?"

"Oh yes and you?"

"I come every day to buy my husband his favorite fruit flan, they are delicious, you should try one." She said smiling and looked ahead to see how many people were ahead of them.

"Oh, I think I'll get one of them too, thanks… I'm Elia."

"Nice to meet you lass, I'm Beatrice, are you new to the area or just passing by?"

"No I live in the old white Victorian house at 501 Bridgeway, on the other side of town."

"Ah, you're a Pearl then." Beatrice looked her over as if to see a family resemblance and the old regal lady looked pensive, "That house used to be lovely in its day, you have some repairs there child, it's been a strange house… many died there."

"Yes, I know"

"I don't mean to scare you Honey, it's just, be careful, will you?" Beatrice implored.

Elia seemed a bit rattled by this, did everyone know about the house and was there talk in the town about her. But as the old lady touched her arm, it felt warm and familiar, and Elia smiled.

"Thank you Beatrice, once I fix it up, I will have you and the whole town up for a housewarming."

"You're sweet, and I would be honored, Miss Pearl. You know I lived there many years ago, I was part of a group of young women that lived there, I knew Prima, she was lovely." There was no phoniness in Beatrice's voice, and Elia felt fondness towards her. They smiled at each other.

"You're next Elia, just again, be careful, that house seems to have a curse and I would hate to see such a lovely young woman like you fall prey to anything dark up there."

"I'm fine thanks, you needn't fret, but thank you ma'am."

"What would you like?" the bakery cashier asked unenthusiastically.

"One fruit flan, thanks, and two French baguettes" Elia replied and paid for her bakery goods.

"Nice to meet you Beatrice" she said with a smile.

"Yes dear, be careful and enjoy that flan. I hope to see you again sometime."

Elia walked away from the bakery not aware of the chatter about her as she left with her groceries. She walked through the streets after putting the groceries in her trunk, and took a stroll. She purchased a large fresh blueberry smoothie, then did her banking and window-shopped nearby.

She wondered about what the old lady said about the house and now she knew that obviously many locals had seen much happen there.

Was it cursed? There was something that Elia was missing, something beneath the surface of what she knew about the house, but how to find out? How to unlock the secrets of the house, and what trouble might come along with that, she had no idea.

She shuddered at that thought. A curse? That would explain the horrible events in that house, but that was only if you believe in curses and Elia did not, she knew she had to dig deeper or find someone to assist her to free this house of its paranormal activity and possibly get answers about her ancestors.

She had done that with Prima years ago, they seemed to have worked it out at the séance, but something else, or someone else was left in the house.

They must have missed something... no, *someone.*

Who was it, and was it evil, would it hurt her, or worse Paul? Would it make Paul hurt her? She had to find out.

She then thought about Paul and forgot about the craziness of her past and the house. Her car was packed with goodies and she decided to drive by where Paul's employer's yacht was, just to see if she could sneak a look at him before tonight.

The water was calm today and the boats just moved slightly under the bright blue sky and sunshine. Nearing the area she pulled the car over and just looked down to see if she could see him.

Elia wanted a sneak peek at her new love, Paul. She wanted to see him in work mode.

There he stood on the yacht, checking the sails as they waved in the sky. He looked handsome and busy, such a manly man. He had no idea that Elia was watching him with a smile of endearment on her face. She watched him talk to the owners with such authority of how to maintain the yacht's appearance and efficiency.

The woman and man seemed very sophisticated drinking wine with their outdoor lunch in their very exclusive yachting attire. Paul continued his job around them like they weren't even there.

Elia watched for a few minutes longer, then drove off to unpack the car.

⚓

Elia stacked the groceries and nibbled slightly on the flan, leaving it for dessert with Paul. It was four in the afternoon and she had to get ready for her somewhat-of-a-boyfriend, or lover, but definitely the man she was in love with. How odd, she had been in relationships before, never for more than a few months, but they never seemed to connect like Paul did with her—this was different, very different.

Above Elia the milky ghost dashed and floated, it was careful not to catch Elia's attention, it was curious to see what she was doing. The table was set on the porch as the night was warm and Elia was dressed in a soft pastel-toned, strapless dress.

"HEY!" came a voice yelling and waving from the front garden.

Elia looked over the porch to see Paul below waving with his right hand while holding a bunch of flowers in his left.

"Hey gorgeous, gate's open, come on up!"

Paul raced up to the porch and held Elia in his arms and kissed her as if he had not seen her in days, instead of just hours.

"You look beautiful tonight Elia."

"Thanks… as do you, handsome," Elia said as she took the flowers from him and smirked as she ran her free hand over his crisp shirt and kissed him more. She quickly dropped the flowers into a pitcher of water on the nearby table.

These two lovers kissed and enjoyed each other's company as the giant moon began to rise and the sun began to set.

The city lights twinkled and the water glistened with its reflection. The air and its warm breeze were back tonight and the evening was perfect.

"This looks delicious again, Elia! Next time I'm taking you out for dinner, my treat" Paul said as he sat down next to Elia. "How was your day?"

"Quiet really, thank goodness. I needed a normal day since arriving here."

"I'm glad, it has been a bit crazy."

"I did chat with this old lady named Beatrice at the bakery and she warned me about the house because she had lived in it years ago and believed it was cursed; that was super uncomfortable for me; everyone in this town knows about the house's history and I only know some of it, doesn't seem fare."

"Beatrice? Oh yes she's a local original and the Grand Dame of Sausalito, and she's probably as old as this house to boot. Don't worry Elia, soon you'll have answers I feel it. We'll be alright here."

Elia served up the casserole and French bread and they ate and chatted about their day, mostly about Paul's eccentric rich employers.

The house wasn't pleased to see sustained happiness within it, and it began to shudder slightly.

"What the hell was that?"

"I don't know Paul, but this house has its moods."

"I don't know if you're crazy or I'm just as crazy, if not more, to be here, knowing this house has these strange occurrences."

"If the house or its paranormal activity wanted me dead or you, it would have happened, I think it needs curing of something to free it."

"Could be, but you have to admit it's bizarre."

Paul opened the wine he had brought and poured two glasses.

"Whatever the situation Elia, I'm here for you," Paul said as he looked into Elia's eyes with importance in his tone.

"Thanks, Babe." As she said this, they both looked at each other surprised at the old-married-couple routine they had worked into so quickly. They laughed together.

"I never thought that coming here on this yacht this time, that I would meet someone who would turn my whole life around, and literally you have, Elia." Paul said.

"Have I? Then that's exceptional! As you are just as much of a surprise to me too, and my feelings are serious."

"My feelings are too, Elia."

Paul cupped Elia's face in his hand as he kissed her tenderly.

The moonlight shone onto the table where small square candles flickered in the breeze around the flowers. The food was eaten and the bread was still being nibbled on. The wine was nearly empty and their kisses were abundant.

"Would you like to stay here with me while your employers are on vacation?"

"I would love to, babe. Some nights we can spend on board just because I do have to watch over it. But maybe I should leave a few things here, you know... if I'm spending time here."

Elia nodded in agreement. "Great, having you here every night with me would be amazing, I would love it."

"Me too. Although I may need to work out a bit more with all of your gourmet cooking."

They both laughed again together.

"How long is the family away for?"

"Eight weeks this time, then they return and I have to sail them back to their home."

"Oh! You mean you won't be working here anymore?"

"Actually... no, but I can try to find another local sailing job Elia. I have been thinking about staying here, there are lots of places to work maybe finally start my own business here. I love Sausalito, so it wouldn't be too hard to stay, if you wanted me to."

"Would you?"

"For you, yes I would, I can totally do that."

Elia sat closer to Paul on the old wicker settee and placed the small blanket over their knees as she drank more wine.

These lovers enjoyed their evening and seemed to be planning their life together. True love was found between them, just like it had found Oshima and Edwin across the ocean in Japan. Now a new beginning and a new life was coming Elia's way and she had no idea how it would turn out, or if she would live long enough to enjoy it.

Chapter 17

*T*he house that seemed haunted by supernatural beings and murderous events had again quieted down from the last few days. No rumblings, nothing. Maybe having told the story of the house, it had calmed it down, and having been free to tell Paul everything was cathartic as well.

Why was it this quiet?

Who were these ghosts?

Why where they there after so many years, gone by?

Nonetheless, Elia and Paul only seemed to use three rooms of this strange paranormal house. They made love in the bedroom, they laughed and ate in the kitchen and they socialized on the outdoor porch.

Paul and Elia had fixed up the bedroom as best they could. It was attired with an antique four-post bed with black Egyptian cotton sheets and a fluffy blue velvet down filled duvet, no man-made polyester blend sheets were to be found here. The silk tufted duvet matched the dozen pillows piled up on the wicker chair under one of the bedroom's larger windows. The curtains were draped to the ground and a translucent fine lace covered the glass.

The solid maple floors had some serious sanding and buffing required, in order to bring them back up to their original beauty.

The rug that covered the floor was losing threads around its perimeter. and it was definitely time to buy a new one. The small side tables matched the four post bed and had a few candles waiting to be lit.

The walls needed a fresh layer of paint as the current wallpaper was faded and out dated, yet the room was peaceful and had old world, antique charm.

The kitchen was abundant with many cupboards and storage nooks for whoever the home's chef was at any time. The old world Viking oven was fully functional and new appliances covered the counter tops.

The exterior porch was just simply breathtaking. Here you could see the town and the bay and the big city on the other side. You could see what everyone was up to around the docks and restaurants, or even relaxing and strolling down Bridgeway.

Seagulls flocked to the rocks lining the edge of the boulevard. They flocked to find small fish and any remnants of food locals left behind near the tourists sightseeing benches.

At night the stillness of the bay was exquisite with the moon over Alcatraz and the stars twinkling on its surface.

The floor of the patio was wood and the furniture was old-world wicker, faded and desperately needing a coat or two of white paint to bring it back to its earlier beauty and shine. Several embroidered and tasseled cream-toned cushions were scattered across the seats and chairs, and the teak coffee table was sturdy albeit weathered.

The mood of the house seemed quiet for now, it shuddered to vibrations of a supernatural existence that for the time being was peaceful and Elia and Paul seemed quite happy to just use these areas of this huge house. The other side of the house lived in peace with them for now. Neither party bothered the other.

Sausalito was awakening to another day of warm summer breezes that seemed to welcome an early morning start. Paul had already left for the boat to do his duties and pack some belongings to return back to Elia tonight and stay with her.

Elia lay in bed, the sheets were warm from a hot summer's night and she was too cozy to move. She smiled thinking about Paul and how he had changed her life. She looked out the window and watched the town below.

Elia then looked around the room, she tried to imagine her relatives living here and what they had experienced by some of the information she had uncovered. She opened her laptop and began searching for more information about her family's name and what contractors she could get in, to try and begin restoring this previously grand-styled home. She had the money, and maybe they would even build a recording studio for her here. Yes, it was all coming together.

Her emails where full of people asking her about the house and her friends that asked when she would be returning back home to LA, business colleagues and her manager were asking about her next album, was she writing? Will she do a show in San Francisco, when was she coming back? She surfed through them answering them all vaguely. She never realized it before, but she did have a lot of friends.

She carried the laptop down to the kitchen, as she surfed the web and ate breakfast; the morning was turning into early afternoon. The scent of eggs and bacon, accompanied with strong black coffee, was dissipating and fading away through the home.

The ghost flew in and watched from above not making itself too visible for Elia to notice. It seemed to like the scent of the home-style cooking aromas and was quiet and comforted.

To Elia's unsuspecting nature she had no idea the ghost was there with her. She typed on the keyboard and searched the internet and kept cross replying to friend's emails.

Strangely, she found she was looking at images of Japan. She watched tourism videos and looked at photos of Japan's landscape and fauna. Its traditions and its rich heritage. She seemed drawn to it. She lost track of where her time was going, and the hours passed by. Elia continued exploring Japan on her laptop. Her black hair shone in the sunlight that now streamed in the kitchen windows, as the sun was slowly setting for the evening.

All of a sudden, a sense of dread came over her, as if she just realized someone else was there. She now had an uneasy feeling that something was awakening in the house, and it made her worry. Something was not right again, and she had a sense of impending doom, or she felt the house was planning something for them. Whatever it was, she would fight it; no one was going to take Paul, or her happiness away from her now... not after all she had been through.

Paul was still on the boat, ensuring it was safe and secure. He had spent the day, cleaning and maintaining it for when his boss would return. He grabbed a large brown leather travelling bag and had begun filling it with his clothes and personal items. He was distracted by the hues of this evening's unbelievable sunset and looked over towards where Elia's house was. He saw a house that needed some work done and saw she was inside and not on the porch. He hurried and packed and locked the cabin before heading back towards the House of Pearl.

Showered and dressed in shorts and a shirt, Elia watched the street below from the porch to see when Paul would arrive. As he approached she felt her heart race quicker and she smiled and waved as he opened the gate and ran up the stairs to meet her.

Chapter 18

Time had passed and the house was still acting up and being crazed. They knew there was still another ghost somewhere, and they knew it wasn't the pirate that killed Oshima.

The two lovers were in the attic and were looking for where the body of Oshima was found. This might give them some clues to follow.

"Oshima's body was found somewhere over here, and the pirate who killed her, was found a few months later under some framing, I think he must have been over there, yeah, right about, there."

Paul looked spooked and jumped back.

"What's wrong Paul, are you scared? You haven't been this quiet since we met."

"Why would I be scared? You said you got rid of the ghosts properly, remember?" Paul shook it off, but he was a bit rattled at being up in the attic that was Oshima's tomb for so long.

"Yes? I think so, but still."

"Well then what's that moving around behind you? Over there in the corner?"

Elia turned and jumped as Paul leapt towards her and yelled, "Boo!"

"Very funny Paul." She turned to look. "Oh my God! I think I saw it too. Let's go back down, now! *Please*."

"Oooh, Look who's scared now."

"Shut-up, Paul and get out of my way. I can't believe this. I can't take any more of this."

Standing behind a trunk Paul yelled to Pearl to help him as he sunk down.

A loud noise pounded through the air and seemed to target Paul, it was pulling him towards it.

"Oh my God it's pulling me into the ceiling! Help!"

"Aaaaaa! " She grabbed his hands and tried to keep him from being sucked into hell-or whatever that thing was. Paul pulled very hard and pulled Elia over the trunk and on top of him for a hug.

"Ha, ha, ha, ha, ha..." Paul said in a voice not his own.

Elia pushed him off of her and he got up. "I hate you! I told you not to do that!"

He tried to hug her as she pushed him away.

"Get away from me," she said, scared and annoyed.

"Hey don't leave me up here alone, after our first fight."

Elia climbed down and left him in the attic alone.

Paul's curiosity got the better of him, and he climbed near the corner where the shimmering image had come from. He shivered as he passed into what felt like a freezer. *So cold.....*

Paul could barely see, and his ankle hit some old wiring and a spray of sparks shot up through his leg. It lit up for a moment what appeared to be an empty sheath of an old Samurai sword.

Paul had a lighter in his pocket and he used it to see as he moved through the smoky attic: it got colder and colder as he got closer to the object of his interest.

He reached out and lifted the sheath with his left hand and brought the lighter closer with his right hand. As these objects got closer the flame was sucked into the sheath and the sheath began to glow, Paul was mesmerized, bringing it closer to his face. Like a drug he had to bring this incredible blue sapphire that was on this sheath closer and closer.

The blue sapphire began to glow and a blue light engulfed Paul's face. Suddenly Paul's face began to morph into the face of the pirate Louie Lorant, and then it morphed back to his own, but this ghost of Louie's was very strong and forceful. Finally Louie took over even though what you saw was Paul's face. Paul's face had been altered slightly by a noticeable scar to indicate his possession by the vile pirate.

While Paul was being taken over upstairs, Elia was outside chatting to a young girl that had just arrived.

"So you say you're looking for Mr. Hamilton? Oh you must mean Paul." Elia responded, and confused a bit.

"Yea he said he'd be here. I talked to him yesterday." The young girl said sweetly.

Elia was curious as to whom this young girl was, and that Paul had mentioned nothing of it. What was he hiding?

"Oh, I left him up in the attic a few minutes ago, I'm not sure if he's come down yet."

Paul appeared climbing down the ladder. His hair was disheveled and his clothes were smoking slightly. He was anxious to share his find with Pearl. His face was still morphing between him and the pirate, with static sparks that occasionally arced off of his body to the blue sapphire. In his hand was the sheath that he had just found in the attic. He went down the hall and out onto the porch and down the front stairs.

"Pearl, Pearl I've got to talk to you! You won't believe what happened up in the attic when you left!"

"Really, Paul, no more games! You're acting like a child!"

"I'm serious, Elia!" His head jerking a bit.

Paul strolled over and greeted his daughter first.

"Bedito?" He said confused.

He sparked and his head jerked again. He had never told Elia about her before and he wasn't nervous now because he was possessed. He cared not that he had kept this a secret from Elia.

"Hi Bedito, honey." He kissed Bedito unemotionally. The little girl looked confused.

"What?" Elia said.

"I just almost died up there and I had some kind of dream or vision! I saw the pirate, and oh, my God! I've got to show you something. Can you open up this old apartment?" Paul pointed to the apartment with the cracked stained glass window.

"Dad?"

Elia Pearl was looking at the two of them with a perplexed and angry glare.

"Dad? What's going on?"

Both Bedito and Elia noticed something different about Paul, he was not himself and seemed like someone else altogether. Paul was not right and they both knew it.

"Elia Pearl meet Bedito, *my* little pearl, I'm sorry I didn't tell you sooner it just didn't come up, with the drama of this house, our romance, your grandmother, the ghosts and besides my ex -wife lives in Mill Valley. This is our love child, so now you know. OK?... Now, open the apartment!"

Paul jumped up without a care about dropping this bombshell.

Elia and Bedito looked at each other, confused.

"What the hell?" Elia said, she tried to understand that Paul had a daughter and he called her his Pearl!

"Just open the door, now, or I'll break it down."

"Hey you're being bossy," Elia brushed his skin with her hand and it sparked violently and she jerked away quickly.

"Are you OK? Did you burn yourself?"

"What's with the sparks? Ouch! What's going on with you?"

"Dad, you're scaring me."

"Sorry honey, but daddy's got to do this one thing."

Elia Pearl fumbled with her keys and opened the door to the apartment that had not been occupied for several decades. Like a possessed zombie, Paul pushed Elia Pearl aside and rushed in first, frantically possessed.

In his rush Paul stumbled over the scattered contents of the small apartment. He fell forward and his hands landed in front of him to break his fall. Under his face was a hatch, so he opened it and in the opened hatch was the exposed head of Louie Lorant with the sword plunged down his throat. Paul pushed himself up to his knees and pulled a carpet aside to reveal more of the gruesome scene.

Paul's face spookily shifted to Louie's for a moment. He slowly pulled the sword out of Louie's mouth. Louie's head shriveled, like a balloon losing its air, and virtually disappeared. There was a sinister sparkle in Paul's eyes as a fierce energy field ran up the sword directly into Paul.

"Oh! No not again, how many of these are there? We've discovered another body!" Elia shuttered.

"What are you two talking about? What is that?" Bedito screamed.

"Since your father has been here I've been telling him stories about this house. People have died here and we thought it wasn't haunted anymore, but there's another body now! Oshima said a pirate killed her but we buried him, this must be Louie Lorant, old Captain Harrison must have found him after all!"

Elia stood dumfounded. Bedito stood shaking with fear and confusion.

"What? Haunted?" Paul's daughter said, not too happy to hear this on her arrival.

"The second body we found was dressed like a coastal pirate. Oshima, the Japanese bride who was almost naked, killed him

171

with a little dagger that we found in her crate, her cut binding was still on her wrists. It was so sad."

Elia had to take a breath, she was winded at the excitement of all this.

"Apparently we thought at the time that his ghost was the angry ghost and the more dangerous one to deal with. Maybe it was this guy all along, Paul, don't you think?"

A glint of evil sparked off of Paul's face as he went in and out of possession by the evil pirate, "Don't worry Bedito and Elia, that old emotionally crippled Captain Edwin came down and showed me the answer. I haven't told you about the dream yet, it was like I was in a movie, like I was really in it."

Paul began to talk again as himself, "I saw Edwin and Louie the foul pirate. Edwin was obsessed with finding him, it was like I was riding on his shoulder and after he talked to every pirate dirt-bag up down the Barbary Coast, he finally got a tip and caught up with Louie at this place called the Clipper Bar. He drugged Louie and brought him back here to the house, and beat him to within an inch of his life knocking out a couple of pieces of the stained glass window with his head, these pieces," and he pointed to the broken stained glass window. Then he slid him down feet first into a hole he dug under the house. Then he impaled him with this awesome sword," he held the sword up.

Bedito and Elia jumped back and ducked as Paul waved the sword around a little more carelessly and definitely out of character.

"After a while, I saw that Edwin was in a rage, and then he skewered the pirate with this sword, impaled him, down his throat, through and through, it was terrible! Louie took a long time to die, that's how Edwin wanted it, but even up to his last words, the pirate swore he would never die and he would live here forever. He said this house was his and no one would stop him."

Paul was looking more evil as the facial scar of Louie was

looking more prominent and the pirate was coming through in him again.

"Paul, you look a little different. What happened to you?" Elia was really scared now.

"Nothing really... I sort of bumped into an old wire... and it kinda electrocuted me... but I'm fine." Paul said, he rolled his neck around, and it cracked very loudly, "And I found this cool sword."

Paul stepped back and shook his head a bit, the pirate was back, "I gotta go 'vache couvir' Heh, heh, heh... If you think you're going to get rid of me, you have another thing coming to you. This is my house and I will be here long after you have rotted in your graves and the worms have eaten your eyes out!! My house, not yours!" Paul yelled, back under the possession of the venomous Lorant.

Bedito looked at Elia quizzically.

"What? Girls?" Paul put the sword in the sheath, strapped it on his back, and rushed off. Paul seemed to be in a different world, that of another time and person. He paid no attention to his daughter or the fact that he never had the nerve to tell Elia about her, and normally that would be a situation anyone would stick around for and would talk it out, with probably many apologies. Instead he just scampered off, and got into Elia's Galaxie and sped off, wheels screeching.

Elia felt responsible for his young daughter and they went back in the house and talked about his behavior. Elia knew better, she knew that he must have been possessed, and they had somehow missed this ghost, it wasn't just Oshima that was here in the house! Didn't Oshima leave when her body was buried? Maybe she needed Oshima now.

⚓

Paul drove her Galaxie throughout North Beach and tried to figure out where his old hideout would be in this future world. The sword was on the seat next to him, and he didn't look the same. He kept mumbling to himself possessed by this ghost.

"Where's my treasure?"

Paul finally located the backside of his old building, and paced quickly up the sidewalk to the front of the building and found that it was "Showgirls," a topless bar and nightclub.

He walked over and awkwardly paid the cover charge, a normal event for the cashier in this kind of place and walked into the darkened venue figuring out how to case the place and find a way down into the sub-basement.

"Showgirls" was a typical, garishly designed strip club with lots of dark corners. Paul picked a darkened corner to sit in and just looked around, and a beautiful, stunning dancer came up to him leaving very little to the imagination.

"Would you like some company?"

"Sure, mon petite vache." Paul answered and again awkwardly accepted the offer of the dancer to give him a lap dance. He then used all of his charms to convince her to help him get down into the lower levels of the building.

The music was loud and thumped. Five stages were lit in amber while each stage had two girls slowly removing their clothes while they swirled up and down on polished brass poles.

One stripper agreed to help him, and guided him through a few doors that she was familiar with, then he found himself in familiar territory and he started to open things that only he could have known were there. They got to a dark and dirty subbasement that no one had been in for a very long time. The music from above had become only a deep and repetitive thump.

Paul found an old broom and swept the dirt floor, eventually he uncovered something like a street manhole cover. He got down on his knees and brushed it with his hands, and blew on it. The notorious logo of Louie Lorant was emblazoned in this bronze cover. Paul's voice was beginning to have a slight French accent.

"Eureka! I have found it. I hope I'm the only one. Let's go inside, huh, follow me."

"Are you sure about this mister?"

"Come on, my sexy girl, this will change your life."

They descended down the ladder into the hole. At the bottom Paul reached into a dark hole in the wall as if he'd done this a thousand times. He turned a lever, and a series of gas lanterns sparked to life around the ceiling perimeter.

An exotic ambience of light cascaded throughout the room. This was a large living suite decorated in Victorian Pirate Plush. The stripper absolutely loved it. She sashayed up to Paul.

"Hey mister can I rent this place? I could make a fortune down here."

"If you help me take some things out of here I'll give you this room."

"Sure, what do you need moved mister?"

"Watch and be awed!" Paul went to one of the heavily decorated walls and twisted a lever, which caused the wall to open, divulging behind it, gold coins stacked to the ceiling.

"OK, I'm awed, and I didn't even have to get naked. I suppose this is what you were talking about that needs to be moved?" The girl said self-importantly.

"Before we go 'mon vache' let's play a little game. Then I'll tell you how we can get this stuff out of here."

Paul spent the night with the stripper, as he was not himself and it was the first night he and Elia were not together since they met.

Elia tried to sleep but she worried all night about Paul, she knew something was not right with him, and he was possessed. She kept wondering where he, not to mention where her car was.

As the young girl Bedito slept on the couch in the nearby room, Elia wondered what the pirate was up to with her beloved Paul. She knew she would have to fight to get him back, and she was ready for anything. They had found each other and she wouldn't lose him now.

Chapter 19

$\mathcal{P}$aul, in the early hours of the morning, with the help of the stripper and a couple of her friends, found a linen truck to transport his treasure back to the house. His stripper entourage helped him load the truck in the back alley and then they followed him back to the house in Sausalito, still not himself. They quickly unloaded his cargo and put it into the lower apartment. The stripper gave Paul a long wet kiss and thanked him for the box of gold coins and drove off with her helpers. When the entourage left the house, Paul saw Elia. He seemed to have transcended back into himself and was trying hard to hold on to his real identity.

"Elia, listen, I'm trying to beat this pirate's possession of me, but can you believe this treasure!" Paul tried to hug her but she pushed him away.

"What treasure? Paul!" She was furious at him, but more at the pirate who was trying to take him away from her. She started to notice a scar appearing on his cheek.

"The captain told me about Louie's treasure, Louie the pirate, well he's in me right now and he wants to take over my body. Elia forgive me! I'm just playing with his spirit, and then I'll throw him out!"

"You can't play with what you don't know about Paul. Have you ever done this before?" Elia was almost in tears and pleaded with Paul.

The scar came back stronger.

"Ah, no, mon petite! That weak little boyfriend of yours is doomed; I will have you and the treasure, and best of all, life again!!!"

"I know this stuff is real, and it can hurt people. Is that how you got these boxes? Did you steal them?" Elia opened one of the boxes. "Oh my God! What have you done?"

He was back to Paul again, and explained, "No, I didn't steal anything. The coins were in this secret vault that Louie had when he was alive, hidden under a building in the old part of the city. I guess nobody ever found it. Now it's ours. We're rich Elia!" Louie came back, and the scar became more prominent along with a glazed look in his eyes.

"But Paul, honey, I'm already rich... we're rich, we don't need this pirate treasure." Elia pleaded with him, but he was Louie again, and there was no way to talk rationally to him.

"You leave my daddy alone!" little Bedito screamed defiantly in defense of her father as she stood in the doorway.

"'Pardon,' I cannot do that. I have been waiting a hundred years for this renaissance of my spirit."

Elia got up and grabbed him by the shoulders.

"No, Paul, Paul, listen to me Paul", she slapped him hard, "You can beat this asshole!"

He hit her right back across the face and she fell back to the floor. Bedito screamed and ran for Elia, but Paul grabbed her by the hair and dragged her into the bathroom kicking and screaming. He locked her in after he loosely tied her with some towels.

Possessed like a crazed fool he went back to Elia who was groggy and tried to get up, he saw what had happened and Paul tried to come through the veil of the pirate.

"Elia, Elia are you alright, oh God, I'm sorry... I can't seem to control this..." he talked to himself like a madman, "Paul? You cannot defeat me, I am one hundred and fifty years old and I have waited a long, long time for this treasure."

Out of nowhere and as it came out of the ceiling, now two fully formed ghosts entered with power and presence like never before, it was Oshima and Edwin. They had returned to try and right the wrongs and protect Elia.

"*But we can*! Now it's our turn to end your miserable existence forever!" Oshima wailed and Edwin snorted as their ghostly figures descended into the room.

Oshima's angry ghost began to morph into a large whirlpool of fire that reached down and wrapped itself around Paul's throat and grabbed Louie's spirit and dragged the evil interloper out of Paul's body right through his head. Paul went into a convulsive state and shuddered uncontrollably. With a dramatic burst of energy, Paul fell to the ground and looked up in time to see Louie swallowed by the blazing whirlpool. He spewed profanities as he was dematerialized and sent to hell by Oshima and Edwin. Paul gasped.

The ghost of Edwin floated above them and spoke to Elia. "He'll be gone forever, and the house will be yours, I must go now Oshima awaits me, you can now have a happy life as I return this House of Pearl to you Elia, use it well. Oshima and I are finally together and we will be happy in eternity. My Pearl and my love..... Thank you Elia......"

Arm in arm, the ghosts of Oshima and Edwin retreated back up through the ceiling, and vanished in a puff of a fluffy white cloud.

"Pearl, baby, Pearl, Elia, are you alright? Say something."

Groggily, "I'm not happy with you."

They then heard some banging.

"Hey let me out of here!" a voice was heard out of nowhere.

"Go get her, Paul!"

Paul jumped up and opened the bathroom door; it was the scared Bedito who panicked and wanted out of the bathroom where Paul had locked her in.

She kicked her dad in the shin, "Don't you ever lock me in a room like that again!" Bedito cried as Paul hugged her closely.

"Ouch! Yes darling, I'm sorry baby, daddy's so, so sorry."

"Come here you two." Elia smiled at the both of them, and the three of them hugged tightly.

Chapter 20

Soon a new day had arrived and even though this house had been the place of many murders, it was now free for them to begin their new life. Paul had an idea, he wanted to take Elia and Bedito out for a leisurely cruise on the bay, to put behind them what they had learned here and what they had seen.

This house had many ugly happenings within it and now it seemed they had found a way out of its darkness and Paul would paint the house with Elia and Bedito. It seemed that they were now in peace and the house was now theirs to restore to its former glory.

The afternoon had ended and the house required more painting and restoring, but for that day, the painting was over as a BBQ was on the plans for them tonight.

Bedito had come to stay with her father for a time as her mother felt he needed to finally be a real dad. The timing couldn't have been better, and the new Paul was ready to settle down with his two favorite girls, and settle down in this resurrected House of Pearl.

"Hey, my two girls, who's up for a day of sailing? My treat! You just have to come and relax with me," Paul asked with a bright tone in his voice, now resolute and happy to live their new life together.

The pancakes had been cooked, the orange juice was squeezed and the two girls emphatically replied yes!

"Then have a hearty breakfast and we head off after we eat!" Paul instructed as he served the hot breakfast.

The sea was calm and the seagulls where back, flocking around the fisherman and their fishing bait. There was enough of a breeze that it filled the sails easily.

A few boats were out that morning and some floated calmly by the yacht. They waved "hello" as mariners always seemed to do. His employers would be back next week and he had to take the yacht out for a routine run to ensure it was in fine mechanical and sailing condition.

They walked along the docks together and laughed. Paul, Elia and Bedito beamed smiles on their faces and anyone around them could tell they were happy to be together. Paul and Elia had chatted at length about the arrival of his daughter Bedito.

Paul had not said much about his personal life to Elia since they met. He had tried to, but that crazy house had priority. Elia had made peace with not knowing as she valued Paul for whom he was, and how he had turned her world into a more loving place. Paul was part of her life now and she loved him unconditionally. Elia and Bedito seemed to get along, and to Paul's delight a new family was coming into being.

Paul held their hands and assisted them on board the magnificent yacht.

After the girls stored the picnic lunch below and the extra fluffy blankets they had brought, they sat on the aft section of the large yacht in a white plush seating area close to the huge stainless steel steering wheel.

After he started the engine and left it in neutral, Paul untied the ropes and pushed the yacht from the guest dock as he put the sailboat into forward gear. After leaving the marina and with enough room to maneuver Paul turned the boat into the wind and ran up the mainsail followed by the jib. He let the boat drop into the wind and the sails filled with a huff and a puff and they were sailing. The loud drone of the twin diesel engines was cut short with the turn of a knob and just like that there was silence except for the rush of water that passed by the hull and the occasional slapping of the sails when they filled with the cool breeze.

Across the bay the yacht streamed further out by Alcatraz where they were now cruising freely.

"Anyone want to have a go at steering? Bedito?" Paul asked proudly, as the man of the boat.

"Sure dad, I'd love too!" Bedito enthusiastically replied, quickly standing in front of her father with her hands on the boat's silver wheel. "Look Elia, I'm sailing this huge boat! Take a picture of me!"

Bedito smiled broadly as Elia fumbled through the picnic hamper searching for the camera.

"Come on Elia!" Pearl yelled out over the waves, wanting this photo to show her friends.

"I got it!" Elia said as she focused the shot, to take the photo. This one simple photo turned into many photos that they would take on the boat that day. It seemed the beginning of a family album had started. Many snap shots were taken. It was a day they would all remember fondly.

"Who's up for lunch now?" Elia asked putting the camera away.

"Sure!" Paul replied. "We'll anchor next to Angel Island and take a break." They made their way there and dropped their sails and their anchor.

"Here's your pastrami roll, Paul," Elia said as she handed it to him with a kiss for the captain.

Paul smiled at Bedito and Elia as they sat there eating their picnic lunch and they looked out at the clear blue skies and the city skyline.

They were free!

They were happy.

They were becoming a new family unit.

"Bet you'd like to stay here more often now Bedito, with your dad and his captain talents," Elia asked affectionately having taken a liking to the young girl.

"I'll be here as much as mom allows me; it's been great to meet you, Elia and to see my dad not with a different woman all the time. I'm glad he met someone nice like you."

"Yes Bedito, I was exactly like that until I met Elia, she's the love of my life, and we're all going to be really happy together," Paul said as he turned to Elia and kissed her.

"Okay that's enough I don't want to puke, Dad," Bedito joked.

"Ha ha! Yeah sure 'Little Pearl,' now grab the wheel and let's turn it into the wind more, we need to move quicker and use the wind."

Paul and Bedito where like two old sailors and loving every moment of it. Elia took more photos of the scenery around them, of the bay and on the yacht; these candid shots were to remember this day.

The yacht sailed faster and took the wind and glided across the bay. It seemed to glide on top of the bay's surface as it sped past other boats. The air blew their hair and their faces beamed with delight. In the distance the horizon glistened with sunshine streaming over the small waves.

Elia was standing near Paul at the wheel, while Bedito sat down on the bow of the ship and felt the speed and breeze and wisps of salt water spray as it blew against her face.

Elia watched Paul and she knew she had to tell him. She had to tell him something she knew would change his life.

She watched him lovingly, looking over to Pearl she knew with a smile on her face that this was the right time to tell him.

Elia moved close to Paul and whispered softly in his ear...

"I'm pregnant."

Paul quickly turned to Elia and kissed her with joy. He was extremely pleased by this.

"You're pregnant... Oh my God, Elia, we are going to be so happy and you won't be alone in that house now, we have our own family!"

"Yes Paul, we are only just beginning our family, and it seems we have a big sister too."

Elia looked over to Bedito and they both smiled. The paranormal forces that had ruined so many lives in that house were now gone.

The house was free, and so was she.....

These three, soon to be four, were free and a new life was now on the horizon for each one of them as they sailed under the Golden Gate Bridge at sunset.

Elia had what she had always wanted, a family that loved her, and she would never, ever, ever, be alone again......

The End

The Authors

Robert Max Bovill

Robert Bovill is a true Renaissance Man from the San Francisco Bay Area. As a Writer, Art Director, Producer, Designer, Scientist, and Adventurer, he mixes his passion for science, design and writing into a career and lifestyle that has earned him numerous awards and praise over the years. As a testimonial to his achievements and success, Robert Bovill has been the recipient of a Gold Broadcast Designers Association Award, and an Emmy Award for Outstanding Individual Achievement in Set Design. Robert's television career has spanned several decades; he has been a longtime Member of the Art Directors Guild, with over thirty years of experience as a professional Art Director in television and film.

His first novel, "The House of Pearl," was inspired by Robert's ownership and renovation of a 120-year old Sausalito waterfront Victorian where his story unfolds. The stories he heard about the house combined with his love of the proud old house; originally built by a sea captain on the waterfront in Sausalito over a century ago, combined with reading about previous tenants and some research at the Sausalito Historical Museum, was the inspiration for the novel as well as his screenplay based on the same story.

At this time, Robert is a partner in 5 Pictures Entertainment, which develops television, film and real estate projects. Robert currently lives in San Francisco with his family. For more information about Robert go to bovillcreative .com.

Susan B. Flanagan

Susan is an Emmy Award® Winning Writer and has won numerous Telly and Aurora Awards for her innovative work as a film and television producer. She is a prolific writer with success in many genres. Her love of storytelling began as a child with a close-knit family that travelled extensively while her father was stationed in the U.S. Air Force. Ultimately settling in Orange County, California, her experiences have become the subject for her novels, films, and television series.

Susan has written numerous feature film scripts, scripted dramas, and unscripted series for television. Additionally she has written several novels, including Escape from O.C. and Shadowlands.

In addition to her creative abilities, her academic achievements include a M.B.A. from Thunderbird Graduate School of International Business Administration, giving her a unique blend of creative and business skills that make her a sought-after talent as both a writer and producer.

Susan lives in Marina del Rey, California.